May·Bird

WARRIOR PRINCESS

May·Bird
WARRIOR PRINCESS

BOOK THREE

Jodi Lynn Anderson

Atheneum Books for Young Readers
New York London Toronto Sydney

Atheneum Books for Young Readers

An imprint of Simon & Schuster Children's Publishing Division

1230 Avenue of the Americas

New York, New York 10020

Book design by Debra Sfetsios

The text for this book is set in Berkeley Old Style.

Manufactured in the United States of America

10 9 8 7 6 5 4

Library of Congress Cataloging-in-Publication Data

Anderson, Jodi Lynn.

May Bird and the bridge of souls / Jodi Lynn Anderson.—1st ed.

p. cm.

"Book Three."

Summary: Three years after her return from the Ever After, May Bird, now thirteen, draws her scattered friends—Pumpkin, Fabbio, Beatrice, and Lucius—out of hiding to take a final stand against Evil Bo Cleevil, as May herself makes ready to live up to the prophecy that placed the fate of the Ever After, and her own world, in her hands.

ISBN-13: 978-0-689-86925-9

ISBN-10: 0-689-86925-8

[1. Fantasy.] I. Title.

PZ7.A53675Maxm 2007

[Fic]—dc22   2007002944

For my grandmothers, Dorothy and Aena

CONTENTS

With Fondest Rememberance

Sarah Burnes—Agent of Divine Inspiration

Liesa Abrams—Soul Mate

Jen Weiss—Dearly Departed Editor

Molly McGuire—Tapping the Walls at Simon & Schuster

Jon Wayshak—Drawing Fresh Blood

Bertrand Comet-Barthe—Generous Spirit
and Purveyor of Fine Chocolates

Lexy James and Erika Loftmann—Luminous Girls

Joe Gouldby, Simone Bechstein, and Zulay Cabezas—
Watchful Presences

Chris Davidson—Ephemeral Poet

And Most of All, My Family—Guiding Stars

THE EVER
NORTH FARM
PETRIFIED PASS
RISK FALLS
PIT OF DESPAIR
STYX STREAMWAY
N
TRAIN TRACKS TO THE FAR NORTH
SOUTHWEST PORTAL
EDGE OF THE WORLD

AFTER

GALAXY GULF

PLATTE OF DESPAIR

BO CLEEVIL'S CASTLE

HIDEOUS HIGHLANDS

NOTHING PLATTE

MYSTERIOUS DOORWAY

PORTO TOWN

HOCUS POCUS

ETHER

HESPERUS

SOUTHERN TERRITORIES

DEAD SEA

BELLE MORTE

Prologue

The night May Bird came home, the cold, bright stars looked down on Briery Swamp, and Briery Swamp—warm as a fuzzy mitten and full of sultry shadows—looked back. Through the trees, the stars had a view of a tiny clearing and a rambling white farmhouse. And the stars could just make out the shadows and faint shouts of joy that issued from the house on one particular night—the night that May Ellen Bird returned home from the world of ghosts.

For May those first days were vivid and bright. Her eyes hugged the dear crooked lines of White Moss Manor. She ran her fingers along the spines of crickets and salamanders, sat under shady trees and in secret hollows, peered into stumps made into frog motels, sank her feet into grass that smelled like the color green, caught leaves the color of October, lay on patches of pine needles with her cat. There were the angles and colors of things alive and bright, not shady and incandescent and deceased. And there was May's mother, Ellen.

Mrs. Bird's cheeks seemed to have grown rosier, her hair had gone softer, her smell had grown sweeter, her voice more warm and rumbly, while May and Somber Kitty had been away. For nights she and May slept side by side, and Mrs. Bird would reach out for her in her sleep and hold her so tight that May promised herself she would never leave home again.

And then, bursting into the quiet bliss of May, her mom, and her cat, were the reporters. They descended on the yard like gypsy moths. May poured out her story to TV cameras, to doctors, to crowds of classmates full of worry and excitement and hope. And—to her great surprise—she was greeted by rolling eyes, snickers into sleeves, and, sometimes, out-and-out laughter.

May met these reactions with bewildered hurt. But it was her mother who hurt her most of all. Mrs. Bird did not snicker, or laugh, or roll her eyes. She only pursed her lips into a tight, worried, disbelieving frown and asked May why, after all they had been through, she couldn't tell the truth.

That was when May stopped talking about the Ever After altogether. It was a long time before her mom, in hopeless frustration, stopped asking.

Sometimes, after Mrs. Bird fell asleep, May would slide out of bed and creep into her own bedroom, still the same as the day she had first left Briery Swamp: hung with photos of far-off places, clothes hangers twisted into animal shapes and strange inventions, and fantastical drawings—of monsters, rainbows, and faeries; of May's first pet cat, Legume, who had died when she was small; and of an odd creature with a pumpkin-shaped head and a mop of yellow hair in a tuft.

Here she would scratch Somber Kitty's ears absently, her eyes trained on the stars outside her bedroom window. As she blinked in the dark, she pictured the shadows of the Ever After, a dusky sky above it full of swiftly passing stars, the starlit stretch of the Hideous Highlands, the oily blackness of the Dead Sea, the purple glow that had surrounded a place called the Carnival at the Edge of the World. Had they needed her there, like they had said they did? Sitting small and thin upon her bed, May could not believe it was true.

And still, one afternoon May found herself sneaking into the woods, Kitty at her side. They made their way beyond the great brier patch, where she knew she would find a lake that made a door between Earth and the world of the dead. But what May found there was not a lake at all. It was only a patch of mud where the lake had been.

She had looked at Kitty and sunk down, fast, as if she had lost her legs.

"Meow? Mew? Meay?" Kitty had inquired.

Any ghost worth its vapor knew that water was the only doorway to the Ever After. And despite the name, it hadn't rained or snowed in Briery Swamp in over a hundred years. Cloudy skies sometimes hung over town with the promise of precipitation—only to scoot along to luckier, wetter towns like Muddy Creek, or Droop Weed, or Skunky Holler.

The lake was gone for good.

May's door to the other world was closed. And although she waited for a sign—a message from the Lady of the snowy north, proof that she was needed after all—nothing came.

• • •

Over time, all grief dulls, and May's was no exception. There were her mother's smiles, there were bike rides with Kitty and icy mornings in the winter and bees sitting on watermelons in the summer and great orange harvest moons in the fall.

And while May's head remembered something else, something before, something glowing, and vast, and doomed, her heart slowly began to forget.

Her telescope in the attic, unused, she failed to see the signs. They came in every shape and size, Las Vegas–style neons, green highway style, some in spotlight letters written across the dark sky, and they were all pointed in the direction of Earth. They were covered in different words, but all to the same import:

WHERE IS SHE?

Word had traveled across the galaxy like a bad game of telephone. But May, fading away like a star herself, didn't hear.

On the windowsill of her bedroom, a cricket said *cheep cheep cheep*. In downtown Briery Swamp, a spider in the rubble of the old post office felt a strange vibration in the atmosphere. At the edge of the White Moss Manor lawn, the woods gaped, its leaves whispering a question to one another every time their shadows touched. *Will she come? Will she come?*

Somewhere far above, the world of ghosts waited.

The seasons rushed through Briery Swamp in great whirling circles, the moon setting in a different place each night, the stars seeming to migrate in circles around the world.

But the whole show was lost on her.

May Ellen Bird had stopped looking up at all.

Part One

A May-Shaped Hole

Chapter One

May Bird Went to the Land of the Dead and All She Brought Me Was This Lousy T-Shirt

In an empty closet in the south bedroom, on the second floor of White Moss Manor, the clothes hangers jangled, as if they had been touched by a cool breeze.

On the bed by the window, swathed in an old quilt, lay two lumps, one girl-sized and one cat-sized. A dark head and a pair of ears poked out from the top of the blanket as the lumps stirred.

May sat up, wondering what had woken her, and crawled out of bed. Skinny as a stick bug and long as a shoelace, May—at age thirteen—was a tall, lanky sort of girl, with legs like a gazelle's and long, graceful arms that seemed a little unsure where they should tuck themselves. The hair that tumbled down her back was black and long. It glistened stubbornly in the cool December air, glossy as silk spun by caterpillars under the moon. Her brown eyes were as wide as windows, but unlike her hair, they barely glistened at all.

Somber Kitty poked his head out from under the covers to gaze at her. Wrinkly and bald, with just the faintest hint of fuzz covering him and batlike ears as big as his pointed head, Somber Kitty was a hairless Rex cat and looked like a cross between melting ice cream and an extraterrestrial. He sneezed before tucking his head back under the covers disgustedly. It was too early. May, gave the closet a curious look, a glimmer of something hopeful in her eye. And then she shook it off, sighed, and began to dress.

Her room had undergone a vast and miraculous transformation in the past three years. Where fantastical pictures used to hang from the walls in sloppy collages, there were now posters of pop stars and favorite movies. Where there had been inventions strewn across her desk, there was now a basket full of makeup, hairspray, and CDs. Only two drawings remained. One of Legume the dead cat. And one of a creature with a lopsided, pumpkin-shaped head. From its spot tucked away in the corner, it watched May's comings and goings with a crooked, ghastly smile.

She pulled on her long johns, then her jeans, and a bright pink sweater. She lifted Kitty out of the bed with one hand, tucked him across her shoulder like a baby, and hopped down the stairs.

White Moss Manor never glowed with homey warmth and good cheer quite the way it did at Christmas. The downstairs hall was filled with the scent of the great pine tree she and her mom had bought and decorated the day before. May slid her socked feet down the crooked, creaky hallway, breathing in the thick smell of fresh holly and evergreen sprigs. She was on her way to the kitchen when she heard a sound coming from behind her down the hall.

She switched directions and sock-slid to the end of the hall, and through the open archway into the library. White Moss

Manor's library was dusty and lopsided, with books lining its shelves from floor to ceiling. The tree lights cast their sparkling reflection across the dusty old book spines and across the couch, where Mrs. Bird lay watching TV.

On the screen, a reporter was sitting in the backyard of White Moss Manor. A ten-year-old May sat beside him, skinny, tiny, and pale, looking so bedraggled she might have just tumbled out of the dryer. The man's hair was slicked back with shiny gel, his mouth open in a big, fake smile.

Ellen Bird looked up at her daughter and scooched back to make room for her. "We can change it if you want, honey. They're doing a Christmas special of their favorite news stories," she said.

"That's okay." May crawled onto the couch beside her mom, and the two curled up to each other like twin caterpillars, Somber Kitty sniffing the crack in between them for a cozy place to snuggle. Sunday mornings at White Moss Manor usually involved eating popcorn and watching a favorite DVD, often *Snow White and the Seven Dwarfs*, which Somber Kitty enjoyed most of all.

No matter how many times she had seen herself on TV, May always found it a bit eerie. She gazed at the image of her ten-year-old self, wondering if she had ever really been that person at all.

"We're here with a girl who needs no introduction. Unless you've been living under a rock the past few weeks, you've seen her—called by many the eighth wonder of the world, her face appearing across the globe on newspapers, magazines, even these"—he held out an armful of paraphernalia, T-shirts printed with MAY BIRD WENT TO THE LAND OF THE DEAD AND ALL SHE BROUGHT ME WAS THIS LOUSY T-SHIRT and squirt bottles labeled EVERLASTING WATER BOTTLE.

"I don't need to tell you that psychiatrists have come thousands of miles to study her. Physicists have examined her hair, her fingernails, even the stuff inside her ears. And still, we're no closer to understanding the mystery: how May Ellen Bird walked into the woods . . . and failed to come out again for three months." The reporter squinted meaningfully.

A growl came from somewhere off-camera, and both May and the reporter looked offscreen, where Somber Kitty had begun to grow restless. May motioned him to shush as the reporter turned back to her, clearly annoyed. "May," he said as he laid down the souvenirs, "tell us: Do you still claim that all those months you were on a journey to the land of the dead, which you say is located"—he turned to the camera—"on a star"—he lowered his voice an octave—"called the Ever After?" He turned back to May Bird, raising one eyebrow dramatically.

May stared at the reporter, then off beyond the camera at Somber Kitty. "Yes."

The reporter cleared his throat.

"And so what you're saying is, there's a world of ghosts up there, terrorized by a fearsome spirit named Evil Knievel, and protected by a wise old 'Lady of North Farm,' who lives in a giant magnolia tree in a snowy valley at the northern edge of the realm?"

May hesitated, then corrected him softly. "It's Evil Bo Cleevil."

"Right, and there in the Ever After, you were assisted by"—

the reporter studied a notepad he pulled out of his pocket—"a ghost with a big squash-shaped head; a girl named Beatrice who died of typhoid in the early 1900s; a deceased Italian air force pilot named Captain Fabbio, who writes bad poetry; and a mischievous, handsome boy named Lucius, your love inter- est. Not to mention your hairless cat." The reporter smirked off-camera, in Kitty's direction.

"Well, I don't have a love interest," May stammered, blush- ing and clearly bewildered.

"And you say you ended up there by falling into a lake that no longer exists"—he nodded over his shoulder—"in the woods behind your house?"

May nodded uncertainly.

"Now, May"—the reporter's smile turned serious—"you have a cult following among people who believe in things like UFOs, yoga, and Bigfoot. Let me run some rumors by you. True or false: Are you carrying the spirit of Bigfoot's two-headed love child?" May shook her head, her brown eyes open wide. "Is Barbra Streisand really Cleopatra reincarnated?" May bit her lip, then shrugged. "Do you believe the reports that appeared in the *Questioner* a few weeks ago that, thanks to your story, NASA is planning to launch a space probe to look for the world of ghosts?" May shook her head.

"May, you claimed that, according to something called *The Book of the Dead*, you're supposed to save the Ever After from certain doom." He looked her up and down intently, as if to indicate the ridiculousness of this claim, given her small stature, her knobby knees, her timid disposition. He leaned forward, and his voice softened dramatically. "If that's true, why haven't the ghosts come back for you? Did they forget you exist?"

Onscreen, the ten-year-old May looked over her shoulder toward the woods behind her. The trees shook and swayed in the breeze, turning up their leaves. They seemed to wave at the camera forlornly. A sad, hurt kind of tilt played at the corners of her lips, and her brown eyes grew even wider. "I don't know," she said.

"Maybe it's because there's no such thing as ghosts?" the reporter asked, smiling obligingly.

May let out a long, soft breath.

The reporter cleared his throat. "One more thing." He looked like he could barely hold back laughter, and he gave the camera a conspiratorial glance. "As our resident expert on the undead, can you tell me what the chances are that zombies might come and take over our shopping malls sometime soon?" He made a dramatic spooky face at the camera and pretended to shiver.

Click. The TV went off.

"Zombies. Of all the ridiculous . . ." Mrs. Bird's voice trailed off as she sat up, arranging her curly brown hair, which had shaped itself into a lopsided lump against the pillow. She shook her head.

May pulled the blankets tighter around herself.

Mrs. Bird looked at her and tilted her head slightly, sympathetic. "Oh, don't look so worried, honey. People forget these things the minute they turn the channel. When you're grown, it will all seem like a distant memory." Mrs. Bird stared at her a moment longer, intently, the way she sometimes did. At times like these, May knew her mom was wishing she could see right into her brain and find the hidden threads of the lost three unbelievable months that were woven there. But to ask again would be to break an unspoken agreement they'd had for years: to never mention May's disappearance—or May's fantastical story of the Ever After—to each other again. It always ended up hurting them too much, because neither could give the other what they wanted.

"Finny Elway called again," Mrs. Bird said, running a finger through May's long hair and pulling it back to braid it, absently. "He certainly is a nice boy on the phone."

May didn't answer. Finny was a boy in her class. Out of all the boys at Hog Wallow Middle, he was probably the cutest and by far the most interesting. He had hazel eyes and brown hair that flopped down in such a way that made the other girls practically faint. And he didn't eat his own boogers, which was a giant bonus. But whenever he called, May pretended to be sleeping, or to have laryngitis, or she would duck under the nearest piece of furniture so her mom wouldn't be able to find her.

"Why don't you go for a walk, honey? It's a beautiful day out."

Mrs. Bird nodded to the window, where pure, white winter sunshine was pouring through. But May only shook her head. She wanted to stay under the blankets with her mom, where it was warm.

Many things had changed for May since she was ten. She had stopped telling bedtime stories to her cat. She had stopped coming home with leaves in her hair and rocks in her pockets, stopped trying to fly by attaching herself to bunches of balloons, stopped dressing Somber Kitty as a warrior cat. And though, truly, she sometimes felt like something inside her had disappeared, it seemed that that must be a natural part of growing up. Standing out too much made one feel too alone to do it forever.

Sometimes, though, when she least expected it, while she was biking to school or out in the car with her mom, watching the woods roll past, or sitting in the rocking chair on the front porch, it came: the feeling that she had let something big and important slip away. And May would whisper to Somber Kitty her deepest secret of all: that sometimes she wished she had never come back from the Ever After at all.

"I'm in the mood for Peanut Butter Kiss cookies," Mrs. Bird said, standing and stretching. She waggled her eyebrows.

May leaped from the couch, sending Somber Kitty tumbling. Naturally, he landed on all fours and yawned, as if he were always getting tumbled off couches.

"Don't mind if we do," May replied. Sometimes, like when she and her mom baked cookies together, May was sure of every reason in the world she had come home.

In the kitchen they turned on the radio and listened to Christmas music, shaking back and forth in unison. Mrs. Bird measured out all the ingredients for the cookies, and May stirred. Some of the batter ended up on May's fingers. She pretended to yawn, wiping it on her mom's rosy right cheek. Her mom stuck a finger in the batter and pretended to fall forward, her battered finger landing on May's nose. Somber Kitty sat on the linoleum floor, swatting his reflection in the glass window of the oven. When the news reports interrupted the music, May grew quiet and looked at her feet, because the news always made her worry—about people who didn't have enough or trees that were being knocked down to build stores. But then the Christmas music was back, and they were dancing again, in a cloud of the scent of baking sugar.

Half an hour later, they had two batches—one of them burnt because they had been too busy pantomiming dashing through the snow to hear the buzzer. May was just putting on the oven mitts to load the third batch when the phone rang.

"Meeeooooow," Somber Kitty growled, staring at the phone, his tail going ramrod straight. May looked at him curiously as Mrs. Bird crossed the room to grab the phone.

"Hello?" she said, once she'd scooped up the receiver. "Hello?" She looked at May, shrugged, and hung up. "No one there. Be right back."

She sashayed out of the kitchen door to the last strains of "Jingle Bells," leaving May giggling behind her. May could hear her footsteps creaking up the old steps and down the hall above. The minute she turned back to the cookies, the phone rang again.

"May, will you get it?" Mrs. Bird called from upstairs. May looked at Kitty. Kitty's tail was still standing straight up. He stared at the phone as if it had grown wings. For a moment, May's heart thrummed. And then she realized how silly that was. Who was she hoping it was. The Bogeyman?

"Somebody would think you'd never heard a phone before," May said, scratching his ears and then walking over to answer it. She pressed her ear against the handset.

She heard only three words . . . and then the line went dead.

May stood, staring at the receiver, a great chill sweeping up and down her body, her ears tingling and a thick lump in her throat. A movement drew her eyes to the doorway, and she jumped.

Mrs. Bird stood there, inquisitive. "Who was it?"

May swallowed. Standing in the doorway now, her mom looked relaxed, content, happy. She thought of before—of her mom's worried looks, and the nights her mom held her so tight, scared of ever losing her again.

"No one," May said, hanging up the phone. "Weird."

Her mom shrugged and crossed the room, pulled the cookie tray off the counter, and loaded it into the hot oven. May watched her, trying to catch her breath.

It couldn't be, of course, what she thought. it had been too long. It belonged to the things that were tucked away.

But the voice on the other end of the line had seemed just like the one that belonged to someone with a pumpkin-shaped head and a crooked, ghastly smile. It had seemed like the voice of a ghost named Pumpkin.

It had said, "We need you."

Chapter Two

A (Bad) Breath from the Past

The most exceptional thing about the town of Hog Wallow, West Virginia—one town over from Briery Swamp—was that nothing exceptional ever happened there at all. Every morning, the Hog Wallow Get & Gallop opened at eight a.m. on the dot to welcome exactly three customers. Every afternoon, Bridey McDrummy sat on her front porch, scowling at her neighbor's poodle, because his exuberant fluffiness seemed to her rather ornery. And every weekday, Hog Wallow Middle School—a long rectangular building perched on a dreary, droopy hill—opened its mud brown double doors to fifty-three students who entered with an air of irrepressible ennui.

The Friday before Christmas, May sat in last-period homeroom awaiting announcements and staring out the window. The school TV program, Channel Smarty, blared from the wall by the door, peppered with ads telling Sister Christopher's eighth-grade class how to get their skin clearer and their hair glossier. Several of the more pimply students in class listened raptly.

May gazed at the lawn outside, thinking—as she had every day since—of that weekend's phone call. More and more, she was convinced she had been mistaken. How would Pumpkin call her from another galaxy? It had probably been a tele-marketer. He had probably been saying something like "We need you . . . to check out this great deal on our new nose-hair trimmer! Only $19.99!" She sighed, resigned. Yes, most likely, the call had been about something as boring as a nose-hair trimmer.

May heard a *thwap* behind her and turned to see that a note had landed on her desk. She looked over at Claire Arneson, whose hair was combed in a perfect ponytail, who seemed to get prettier every day, who was always changing to turquoise nail polish when everyone else had just made the switch to fuschia. Claire gave her a secret wave. May smiled back and unfolded her note on her lap.

Will you sign this for my cousin? was all it said. May dug for a pen in her desk.

Being a celebrity had made May something of a sensation at her school, and after three years that still hadn't faded. After all, the only other time anyone from Hog Wallow had made the news was when Jebediah Hickorybutte had gotten a moth stuck in his ear in 1987 and penned the fated-to-be-famous poem "What's that you say? I could not hear. You see, I have a moth in my ear."

Since the day she had first appeared on TV, May had been treated like Hog Wallow royalty—of a sort. She was always asked to sit with the other girls at lunch and was always included in parties. She was even asked, from time to time, to autograph notebooks, or lunch bags, or shirt collars.

But being popular also seemed to come with lots of rules May hadn't anticipated. In gym class she had to make sure to run slower than all the boys, because Peter Kelly had insisted girls were *supposed* to be slow. In library class, Claire insisted she read books like *Kissing Boys at the Beach* when she really wanted to read about Egyptian mummies or space travel. May sometimes felt like she was fitting herself into a smaller and smaller box. But it seemed better than being a weirdo who used balloons to try to fly. It was easier, at least.

May Bird. May signed the note from Claire and looked up, just happening to meet the hazel eyes of Finny Elway. She frowned at him and looked away. She tried to look as bored as possible.

For the most part, boys were scared of May. It was the way she had grown over the years, into that kind of prettiness that wasn't so easy to see. It was the way her dark hair glinted like a wild cat's, and it was her mysterious connections—however little anyone actually believed in them—with ghosts. But truly, the fear was mutual. May knew she wanted a boyfriend *one* day. But how did you ask a boy out, anyway? How did you keep it together if one asked *you* out? How did people kiss? It made her think wistfully of how easy, in many ways, things were for ghosts. Life held so many challenges that the land of the dead did not.

"May, didn't you have an announcement?"

Biting her lip, May stuffed Claire's note into her desk quick as a flash and looked at Sister Christopher, standing in her brown nun's habit and staring at her expectantly. She slid out of her desk and shuffled to the front of the room. "I just wanted to remind everyone about my birthday party tomorrow," she said, feeling shy. It was her first ever real birthday party . . . aside from the ones attended only by cats named

Legume or Somber Kitty. In fact, it was Somber Kitty who had talked her into this one by dragging his old party hat out of May's closet and carrying it around like a kitten, meowing pitifully. If Somber Kitty didn't have some fun soon, May feared he would be lost in a sea of melancholy forever.

Excited whispers rustled through the room—everyone wanted to get a glimpse inside her mysterious, rambling house after all this time. As Sister Christopher stepped forward to continue afternoon announcements, May drifted by the teacher's desk on her way back to her seat. But halfway past, she froze.

On the middle of the nun's desk was a newspaper. On the front page was an old, grainy black-and-white photo of someone May knew very well—a ghastly looking woman with rotted teeth. May reached out and pulled the paper to her, swimming in goose bumps. MYSTERY OF DISAPPEARANCES STILL UNSOLVED AFTER MORE THAN A HUNDRED YEARS. And under the photo, the caption: "One of the victims: Bertha Brettwaller, known for winning personality and bad breath, who disappeared shortly after the Hog Wallow hoedown in October 1897."

There were other pictures beneath Bertha's. One of a group of twelve miners who, the caption explained, had inexplicably drowned in a lake in the woods. One of three nuns who had disappeared after skipping off into the same woods twenty-five years before. And then May caught something else, out of the corner of her eye, that made her start. There, at the top right-hand corner of the paper, where the date was supposed to be, were these words: "Be ready." And the unmistakeable eyes of the Lady of North Farm printed above them.

May dropped the paper. When she looked up at the corner again, the words were gone. If it hadn't been for the phone call from a few days before, she would have thought she'd imagined it.

And then she heard the squeal of desks behind her. She turned to find the whole class chattering excitedly, running to the windows. May walked toward them slowly, afraid of what they were all looking at, of what she might see outside. Every child in the eighth grade had their noses pressed against the windows, looking at the sky. May leaned forward and looked up too, but she saw nothing but a gloomy sheet of white clouds.

"What's going on?" she asked Peter Kelly.

"Didn't you hear Sister Christopher?" Claire sang.

May shook her head. Claire nodded to the sky, a giant grin spreading over her face.

"It's amazing."

"What?" May asked, following Claire's eyes, bewildered.

"Where have you been, May? In outer space? They're predicting snow!"

Chapter Three

First Snow

The day of her birthday party, May woke to a strange smell in the air. She blinked, sat up, and looked out the window. Great gray clouds draped the sky above. The trees stood gaggled together in the woods, perfectly still, as if in anticipation of something . . . big. The birds had disappeared, and the whole world seemed to be wrapped in a waiting sort of hush.

And then it happened. It drifted side to side like a feather, falling to the world below in slow motion. A snowflake.

May gasped. She leaned forward and pressed her face to the glass. Another tufty flake fell past her window, then another.

"They're coming for us, Kitty," she whispered. "They have to be."

Beside her there was a rustle under the covers. Somber Kitty's ears, poking out, tilted and turned like satellites. And then the rest of his body emerged, shaking and twisting itself and lengthening out in a long, taffylike stretch. He yawned, sneezed, and licked his chops, looking at May bemusedly. And then he placed his paws on the windowsill beside her. When he saw the tiny white crystals—several now—drifting through the sky like plummeting moths, he let out another yawn, clearly unimpressed.

"No time to waste," May said.

She hopped out of bed and made her shivering way across the room to her closet, opening the door quietly so as not to wake her mom down the hall.

There, on the floor where it had sat collecting dust for years, was a cardboard box. She knelt beside it, pulling open the flaps and reaching inside. She took hold of a piece of fabric and lifted her black bathing suit into the air in front of her. In the Ever After, it had glowed with swirling galaxies and supernovas. Now it was just a plain black bathing suit with silver sparkles. But it was reassuring to May, just now, to know that it was still here, tucked safely away. She laid it down, next sinking her hands into the soft velvety fabric of a garment that looked a lot like a cape with a hood—her death shroud. In the Ever After, it had been the thing that made her—a vibrant, living girl, or "Live One" as the living were called—look as deceased, filmy, and gray as the next specter. It, too, looked like an ordinary lump of fabric now. May patted it gently and replaced it, lovingly, into the box.

She looked over her shoulder at Somber Kitty, who lay on the bed watching her, still as a stone sphinx.

"C'mon, Kitty," she said, pulling him off the bed like a string of spaghetti and hanging him over her shoulder. "We need to be ready."

By that evening, Briery Swamp was blanketed by a thick layer of pure white snow. Through the windows, it looked like a whole different world—one coated in marshmallow frosting. May scurried about the Manor getting ready for her guests to arrive, just to have something to do for herself. Three years before, she would have paid the world's riches to be having her very own well-attended birthday party. But suddenly she didn't care very much about the party at all. She hung balloons, a disco ball her mom had bought in Hog Wallow, and two piñatas she and her mom had made, and then she started in on baking cookies—the whole while stopping at every window to gaze at the woods or peer into the clouds above, as if the Lady of North Farm herself might suddenly appear there. Across the front yard, under the canopies of trees, were dark spaces that seemed to beckon, promise, whisper. Somber Kitty lay draped around her neck, on guard, his tail clothes-hanger straight. Anticipation fluttered about the house like a clutch of butterflies. It landed on everything May touched.

Knock, knock, knock!

Both May and Kitty jumped at the sound of the door at three p.m. sharp. Mrs. Bird, who'd been helping in the kitchen, gave them both a look as she walked into the hall, wiping her hands on a dishcloth. "Nobody's going to get that?" she said, shaking her head and pulling on the doorknob.

There, bathed in white, were Claire Arneson, Maribeth Stuller, and Mariruth LeTourneau, their cheeks rosy, snow bouncing off their hats and stuck to the fabric of their mittens. They burst inside, pouring gifts into May's arms at the same time they poured out waves of chatter.

"Can you believe it's snowing? How long do you think it will last? Do you think we'll be off from school?"

After that the guests arrived in bucketfuls, all brimming with the same bright talk, all wide-eyed at their first glimpse inside White Moss Manor, though of course they had all seen it on TV. There was a great stamping of boots in the hallway, a loud shuffling of stockinged feet on the creaky old manor floors, a great clinking of mugs of hot cider in the kitchen, oohs and ahhs at the house's great halls and staircases, at the disco ball, and at the cookies May and her mom had made: raspberry-chocolate, violet-mint, peanut butter-banana—all recipes May had created.

May smiled a lot at everyone, like a good host, but it was like wearing a mask. She was dying to tell someone the truth. But she had learned from experience that she was the last thing they wanted to hear. Mrs. Bird had cooked May's favorite home-made lasagna, and they all gathered around the table to eat, laughing and honking at one another happily. May sat at the head of the table, feeling almost like an observer instead of the guest of honor. Her mother set the casserole dish on the table, beaming at her proudly as if they had reached the pinnacle of happiness.

May smiled back, but her eyes drifted beyond the table to the snow outside. She sat on her hands and tried to contain her excitement. She kicked her feet back and forth against the linoleum, her coltish legs too long for the chair. Finally she couldn't sit another minute. "I'll be right back." She popped up from the table and headed up the narrow old stairway to the upstairs hall. She walked into the bathroom, closed the door, and stood in front of the sink. She washed her face. She straightened up, looking at herself in the mirror, smiling hopefully.

The lights flickered.

May jumped, turned her back to the mirror, and looked around. Fear, absent a moment before, sent shivers racing up her spine. She stood still for a moment, breathing fast, staring about the room. She strained her ears for a moment, then, hearing nothing, reached for the handle and slowly tiptoed out into the hall.

For a moment the hallway lights glowed extra bright, and then they flickered again. The next moment they were out completely.

May swallowed, taking a few more slow steps down the hall and listening hard. "Pumpkin?" she whispered. She could hear the sound of her own heart beating. But nothing else. "Is it"— she gulped loudly—"is it you?"

She stepped toward the stairs and . . .

"Ah!"

Somber Kitty leaped out of the shadows, flapping his tail at her. "Meay?" he asked, tapping her shin with his paw, clearly wanting to be carried.

May shook her head at him, silently chiding him for scaring her, and then scooped him up into her arms and held him tight. Together they drifted down the stairs.

When they appeared in the doorway of the kitchen a few moments later, they must have been a sight. May was as pale as a ghost. Somber Kitty had crawled around her neck, his tail straight as a pencil, his fuzz sticking straight up, a worried look on his face. The table, which had been full of chatter a moment before, fell silent as everyone turned to look at them.

"May, are you okay?" Claire asked. May looked at her

mom, who was leaning against the kitchen counter. Their eyes met.

At that moment the phone rang.

Mrs. Bird looked at the phone, then at May. She reached for the phone and picked it up, staring at May curiously, clearly not hearing anything on the other end of the line.

May swallowed. "It's the ghosts, Mom," she said, looking around the room, embarrassed that every face was intent on hers. She cleared her throat and went on. "They're trying to reach me from the other side." She straightened her shoulders. "They're coming for me."

The screams that issued from White Moss Manor were the loudest in Briery Swamp history. May's friends exploded out of the house like fireworks, in a wave of high-pitched squeals, pouring onto the front lawn, scattering to the farthest reaches of the yard and screaming for their parents, shivering wildly without their coats and hats.

The party ended in record time. Within half an hour, the parents of Hog Wallow had descended on White Moss Manor, taken their children, and left.

The last person to depart the premises was Claire Arneson. May stood on the porch to say good-bye, but Claire, her ponytail bouncing frantically as she ducked into her dad's SUV, didn't look back once. May watched her go, her hand up in the air in an unseen wave. She was pretty sure it was her last birthday party.

Inside, her mom sat in the kitchen with a cup of tea, surrounded by plates full of the half-eaten lasagna she'd made, the balloons she'd taped to the walls, the piles of uneaten cookies she and May had baked. The look on her face as May walked in was enough to fill May with shame.

"I'm sorry, Mom, but—"

Mrs. Bird held up her hand in a "stop" motion. "Not now, May."

May stomped up the stairs, Somber Kitty trailing behind her with his tail between his legs. It wasn't fair. She was only telling the truth. Once they were tucked in her room, she pulled the box out her closet. She pulled out her bathing suit and her death shroud, rebelliously shedding her party clothes in one smooth motion and shrugging into the others in the next. The bathing suit stretched to fit. Feeling cold, she pulled on her warm fuzzy pajama pants and her sneakers and turned to look in the mirror. She looked like a girl playing dress-up. But she also looked ready.

May put Kitty's shroud on him, too, and then she waited. And waited. The minutes ticked by, and nothing happened. It began to get dark outside.

When the phone rang at nine, May nearly jumped out of her skin. She ran to her doorway and listened as her mom picked it up. A few minutes later Mrs. Bird appeared at the stairway. She stopped halfway up when she saw May watching her.

"What are you wearing?" she asked, staring at the shroud and the bathing suit.

May looked down at herself. "Just . . . um . . . messing around?"

Ellen sighed, sounding exhausted. "It was the phone company. Apparently our line's been spliced for a week with some-one's in Hog Wallow. A pizza delivery place . . ."

May stood, transfixed. *We need you* . . . to bring us a large pepperoni? Her heart nearly sank through the floor.

"Sounds like people all over Hog Wallow have lost power because of the storm too."

May was quiet as a stone. Had she imagined it all? Pumpkin's voice? Did that mean she had imagined the words at the top of the newspaper, too? Ellen gave her a searching look, then walked up the rest of the stairs to May. "Let's forget about this and go back to normal in the morning, okay, honey?"

She bent over and kissed May's cheek, engulfing her in her warm, familiar jasmine smell. May sank into her hug.

"I want you to go straight to bed."

"Okay, Mom." May felt very small.

"Hey." Ellen touched her cheek. "You're my girl, no matter what. Don't forget that. I don't know what I'd do without you."

May nodded. She watched as her mom walked down the hall and disappeared into her room.

Could it be? Could it be that it was nothing? Would she stay here in Briery Swamp with most of her heart tucked into shadows?

Standing in the hallway, with her mind light-years away, in a snowy forest at the northern edge of the world of ghosts, she was a sort of May-shaped hole. It seemed that for all her life, she would feel like she belonged in neither one place nor the other.

She would only ever belong somewhere in between.

Chapter Four

Widow's Walk

eay." In the dark, later that night, Somber Kitty crawled onto May's lap. The shutters banged with the storm outside. The trees swayed, lit dimly by the moon behind the clouds. The snow pattered against the windows in great diagonal specks.

May listened to the sounds of her mom getting ready for bed and then closing her bedroom door. She stood up and crept into the hallway, to the door that led to the attic. Slowly, carefully, she pulled it open and climbed the stairs.

The attic of White Moss Manor was narrow, dark, and dusty. May tiptoed across the slatted wooden floor and sank next to her telescope, which was covered in a fine layer of dust from years of neglect. She stared out the window at the woods. The trees swayed back and forth in the snowy breeze.

On one side of the room was a ladder that led to a widow's walk—a sort of thin, railed walkway that crossed the roof of the house. May looked at it. She hesitated only a moment.

The hatch was rusty, but with a great push, May managed to push it up, and it swung open with a clatter. She paused, listening for any sounds of her mom below. The world above was muffled with snow.

"Yow!" she hissed. Kitty had tapped her heel with his paws, not wanting to be forgotten. She scooped him up, stuffing him under her shroud.

May rose gingerly, trembling, until she was fully outside, enveloped in the cold air. The wind felt like it was blowing right through her bones. She stepped carefully along the widow's walk, all the way to the edge of the roof where it ended, and peered down at her front yard and the woods beyond. They looked so far below that May, who was scared of heights, got a little woozy. She looked up at the sky instead. Her heart began to tear and ache.

And then all the thoughts she'd been ignoring for so long flooded in on her. Were they okay? Were her friends in the Ever After okay? Had she let them down? Had they forgotten her?

"Where are you?" she said to the sky. Tears gathered in her eyes, and the wind blew them sideways.

The clouds roiled. The sky blew. The snow on the lawn lifted in clouds and blew here and there in tiny, tornado-like swirls. In the clouds of white May thought she could see ghosts, faces and shapes of the dead all around her. She held Kitty tight in her arms and kept her face turned up to the sky, as if waiting for someone to descend from the storm clouds and lift her away.

And then a strong gust blew against her, and her feet slipped just slightly. She jerked forward against the railing, ever so softly. But, rotten, it crumbled like paper, and May and Kitty went sliding forward, right through it. May scrambled to stop herself, but it was too late.

They slid a few more feet, then fell off the edge of the roof.

They looked like blackbirds falling through the sky.

Part Two

Bo Cleevil Is Number One!

Chapter Five

An Empty Shore

"M eow."

May sat up, rubbing the back of her head.

"Mew."

Kitty must be lost in the snow. She scooted onto her knees to look for him, and then discovered that there was no snow. She looked up. There was no front lawn. There was no White Moss Manor.

Where was she? She peered around. They were in the woods. They were in the clearing where the lake used to be. Where the lake . . . was!

The lake was there, in front of her. May gaped at it, its dark water glimmering.

"Meay."

May whipped around to see Kitty, sitting by an open doorway that stood in the middle of thin air. He was floating, and eerily translucent.

"Kitty, your death shroud's work—" May stopped short as she looked down at herself. Her death shroud was working too. She had the thin, ghostly glow of the dead.

A firefly landed on her cheek, and she brushed it away,

dazed. She stared back at the door again. They weren't in the woods behind her house. They were in the woods on the other side!

Slowly May got to her feet and almost lost her balance as they floated out from under her. She threw out her arms to steady herself, letting her legs dangle loosely, trying to get used to the feeling of levitating. She floated toward the door, her heart thudding wildly in her chest. Were they really here? Could it be real?

The door stood open, just a crack. May looked behind her to the lake, which used to hold a vicious water demon lurking in its depths. But now nothing stirred. She looked back at the door, which used to be locked, only to be opened by a secret knock. She bit her thumbnail.

Uncertain, she lifted Kitty into her arms and tucked him underneath her shroud, knowing how dangerous it could be for him, since all animals had been banished from the Ever After, to nobody knew where. She pulled the door a little wider and drifted inside.

The hallway ahead flickered with blue light coming from a doorway a few feet away. May drifted to it—she knew it was an old movie theater that welcomed all recently deceased spirits to the world of the dead. She hovered in the doorway, peering inside, surprised to see that all the seats were empty. On the screen, instead of the morbid specter who'd appeared there last time, orienting spirits to the afterlife, there was a goblin, its big ears waggling, its teeth glinting, wearing a strapless evening gown and Gucci sunglasses.

"Hgglblblebe," it said. "Bluggblebleebgg Hllbggguu." Translations in several languages ran across the bottom of the screen. "Welcome to Planet Cleevil," May read breathlessly, "where everything is very organized, and you never have to worry about anything, because nothing means very much." May watched in shock as the goblin went on to explain that there were many places to go shopping.

Finally the movie ended with a great flapping of the film projector somewhere above. May hesitated a moment, composing herself, and then floated farther down the hall, pushing—with some dread—through the door marked EXIT.

Here she felt her stomach flop sickly. The immense beach, butted along the far side by the dark waters of the Styx Streamway, was the same as she remembered. It was an endless stretch of sandy shore, with rowboats docked along its edges waiting to take the newly dead to far-off destinations all over the realm. Streams stretched out from the river's mouth, marked with signs such as SOUTHERN TERRITORIES, NOTHING PLATTE AND THE FAR WEST, DEATH KNELLS, NEW EGYPT, PIT OF DESPAIR AMUSEMENT PARK.

But the beach no longer bustled with thousands of newly dead souls being ushered to various destinations all over the realm. There was not a soul in sight. The shore was deserted.

"Meay?" Kitty whispered through May's collar.

"Shhh," May whispered. There was something else different that she couldn't put her finger on. And then she looked up. There were no stars zipping through the sky above at lightning speed, like comets. The stars were gone. No, the *sky* was gone. There was only a low, dark cloud where the sky used to be.

May turned to look back at where she'd come from, but now

there was only a brick wall where the exit had been, marked with the glowing letters SPECTROPLEX. A sign up near the top announced in neon: YOU'LL NEVER GET OUT AGAIN. HAVE A NICE DAY. Beside it, in big, bright red letters, was scrawled "BO CLEEVIL IS NUMBER ONE!"

May turned back to look at the Streamway, grasping her situation.

She knew from experience that there was no way to go backward. But she didn't know which way to go forward, either. The last time she had seen her friends had been in South Place, thousands of miles away, with a horde of goblins, ghouls, and zombies—all of the realm's dark spirits—at their heels. She was certain that Lucius—a luminous and wily boy—had made sure they escaped. But to where?

And . . . how *had* she gotten here, anyway?

No one had appeared before her on the roof of White Moss Manor. She had seen neither hide nor hair of a spirit coming to show her the way.

"It's the Lady," she whispered. The Lady had somehow brought her back. And now she just needed to wait for a sign to point her in the right direction.

May stood still, examining the clouds, the brick wall behind her, the sand, the water, waiting for a message.

"Hblbglblgbgl." She whipped around. The sound was coming from the Spectroplex. The sound of ghouls.

"Hglbelblbeeee."

In her shroud, Kitty began to shiver. Well, she couldn't stay here.

May could really think of only one place to go. It was the one place she was sure that, if he could, Pumpkin would go.

She turned and hurried toward one of the boats bobbing in the shallows of the Styx and laid Kitty gently on its floor. She then took a good look across the water, squinted, and grasped the stern, giving it a running shove and then leaping inside.

Kitty stood to watch as the boat moved away from the shore, his paws up on the bow, meowing a protest against the water. On the beach, the dark figures of about ten ghouls appeared, and May pulled him down to duck. They stayed like that for several minutes, until the shore was gone from sight.

As they drifted into the shadows, the area around them seemed to have gone completely silent. In fact, it felt like they were the only two creatures left in the world.

They floated past a sign that hung overhead. It read, in drippy letters, BELLE MORTE, 1,300,017 MILES.

Chapter Six

Back to Belle Morte

From the water, Belle Morte reminded one of a sleepy old miser, perched up ahead on either side of the stream, its gray stone houses curvy and slumped as if they had used up all their energy just being built at all. In the gloom, dim lights glowed in the yellowed windows of the old stone halls and shops and reflected on the dark water of the stream. May pulled Kitty under her shroud.

The boat drifted under a small stone bridge, steering itself toward the right-hand side, where it bumped gently against the dock.

May climbed ashore, keeping her face lowered. The last time she had been seen in Belle Morte, the whole town had gone into an uproar over a Live One being in their midst. May hoped that this time, wearing a handmade death shroud from North Farm itself that made her look as ghostly as any spirit one might see in a graveyard on a Saturday night, no one would recognize her. She peered left and right. To either side of her, stone houses cozied up against the walkway, tilting overhead with their drippy, triangular roofs. But not a spirit occupied the paths along the banks of the river. It felt as if it could be early morning, before anyone had risen.

May felt the rumblings of worry, but she tried to ignore her unease.

The shops along the Streamway were deserted. Chains and souvenirs had been left lying on the road. Doors hung crookedly ajar, OPEN signs still dangling in their windows: Coffin Coffees, Mortician's Magic Beauty Parlor, Chokey's Chocolates—its window still full of delectable treats such as tiny chocolate coffins opened to reveal tiny chocolate skeletons inside. Hearses and carriages stood empty, their doors wide open. And above it all stretched the same dark cloud she had seen at the Spectroplex.

May's heart thudded. The last time she'd been here, the streets had been full of bustling, happy spirits of Belle Morte— dead Pompeiians gleefully leaping out of the Towering Inferno Hotel, gooey ghosts out shopping and chatting mournfully, sinister-looking murderesses sweeping the crowds with menacing glances, specters in all stages of decay, and dimly glowing house ghosts. They were all gone.

May drifted through the back door of the Moldy Page Bookshop, brushing cobwebs out of the air in front of her face and sneezing at the dust. On the counter by the old metal cash register, a book lay waiting to be purchased: *A Farewell to My Arms*. The amount had already been rung up on the old metal cash register, and its drawer hung open, full of gold coins.

She floated uncertainly to the front of the store, where a door opened onto the main square of Belle Morte. As she emerged, she saw a structure toward the edge of the square, where Main Street began its journey out of the center of town. A shiver went through her.

COMING SOON! CLEEVILVILLE #786

PARDON OUR DUST!

COMING ATTRACTIONS: CRAWL-MART,

CHAR-BUCKS, SKULLBUSTER VIDEO

"Euggggggggh."

May ducked back through the doorway, clutching Kitty tight. She watched as a group of zombies lurched across the far side of the square—their bloodthirsty yet dimwitted eyes scanning the area for any stray spirits, their clothes tattered, their greenish gray arms sticking straight out ahead of them and their legs jerking them along lopsidedly. Another group, she could see now, was gathered at the Char-Bucks— which was only half-built—sipping steaming drinks and *Eugggghhhhh*ing at each other. "Euggggghhhhh" was the only word in the zombie vocabulary.

"Pumpkin," May breathed, her lips trembling. The dark spirits had taken over his hometown.

Her eyes shot to an old Victorian bicycle—basket and all— lying on the ground a few feet away. Watching the zombies in Char-Bucks, she scurried over and lifted it up, dumped Kitty gracelessly into the basket on the front, and climbed on. She wobbled and swerved as the bike floated along, several inches above the ground, finally setting a straight course up Main Street. She began to pedal furiously. Within a few moments the town had fallen far behind them.

Beehive House sat all by its lonesome in the middle of the sand, light glowing from its windows. It looked perfectly intact, perfectly still and peaceful. May skidded to a stop, taking a deep breath. But when she saw that the front door stood wide open, she felt a new wave of panic. She and Kitty looked at each other. "Meay?" he asked.

May walked warily toward the door, Somber Kitty at her heels. She stepped into the open doorway, into the shadow of the threshold. "Hello?"

Finally she pushed the door the rest of the way open and stepped all the way in. "Oh." She sighed.

When May had last been to Beehive House, it had been a cozy dwelling, inhabited by Arista, a bookish, puttering bee-keeper and master of the house. Pumpkin, who was a certain type of spirit called a house ghost, had been his servant, but not a very industrious one. The house had been on the clut-tered side. But now it was in chaos—books and papers were strewn across the floor. May walked through the kitchen, into the study, where Arista's skull-o-phone hung off the hook. "If you'd like to make a call, please press the anterior bicuspid and dial again," it said, over and over again. Arista's maps had been torn up, and his globe of the universe, which showed what all the stars and planets were and how many spirits lived on each, was cracked down the middle like a hard-boiled egg, but still blinking and twinkling. There were brochures for Rot-ten Roxie's Roller Rink and Remaining Fingers Nail Salon, mixed among a pile of newspaper clippings from the *Daily Boos*. May sifted through them, reading the headlines, the words brightening to a distinct green glow as her eyes touched them:

DARK SPIRITS TAKE OVER REALM, CURIOSITY GROWS
OVER RASH OF TACKY STRIP MALLS LEFT IN THEIR WAKE

HOPES OF SALVATION BY LIVING GIRL

DASHED BY HER DISAPPEARANCE

THOUSANDS OF VANISHED SPIRITS RUMORED

TO BE KEPT IN BO CLEEVIL'S BASEMENT

REPORTER VANISHES AFTER REPORTING ON

SPIRITS KEPT IN BO CLEEVIL'S BASEMENT

The next article was just a blank page.

May scanned the papers again, hoping that maybe here she would find some sign from the Lady of North Farm, like she thought she'd seen at school in Hog Wallow. But there was nothing. She laid them down, thoughtful. She drifted back to the kitchen, and then into the guest bedroom, where she had spent her first lonely, scary night in the Ever After. The sheets of the bed, ratty and decayed in the first place, had been torn up. Somber Kitty leaped onto the bed and sniffed around.

As she went back into the kitchen again, she caught a glimpse out of the corner of her eye of something moving. She swiveled toward it, then breathed a sigh of relief. It was only her reflection in the mirror—in her death shroud. Tall, lanky, long-haired, and disheveled, she looked far different from the little girl who had stood in Arista's house three years before. Then, she hadn't known about Bo Cleevil at all, or ghosts for that matter. She had been terrified of Pumpkin. She hadn't known he had been haunting her house all her life, watching over her, invisible.

"Pumpkin's grave," she whispered, and rushed out of the house. Pumpkin's grave wasn't hard to find, it sat just beyond the beehive in Arista's garden, a big rectangle in the ground with a slab of stone on top engraved with his name. Spirits in the Ever After used their graves as doorways to haunt the Earth—all very routine and proper. There were countless graves gathered around all the towns for this purpose. Though if you tried to use someone else's grave (or just fell in by mistake), you ended up as a lost soul, doomed to drift about the universe alone forever and ever.

She gave the stone slab a shove and peered inside. But only a gaping rectangle stared back at her.

But no, there was something else. A black lump, just in the corner.

May reached in and lifted it up. A bow and a quiver of silver arrows. Her bow and arrows. Pumpkin had expected her to come back! The bow had once felt awkward on her, but now she shouldered it without a moment's thought.

She floated back indoors, into Arista's study. She stood in front of the broken globe, tracing with her finger a line between the star called the Ever After and the planet Earth. Not knowing what else to do, she settled in for the night, poring over a map of the Ever After, wondering what to do, where to go. Her finger, tracing the map, landed on the capital city of the realm, Ether. Ether was an ancient city, and the Eternal Edifice, in the center of the city, was the oldest in the realm, as old as the Ever After itself. The Edifice was guarded by the magic of the Lady herself, along with the high ghost court. Most especially because it contained *The Book of the Dead*, which held all the answers to the universe.

No matter what happened in the Ever After, May was sure that the Eternal Edifice was safe.

She sank onto her elbows. When she looked up from under her eyebrows, she noticed something glowing red under the map, and lifted it.

There, underneath, was a piece of paper, carefully folded and pulsing with red light. Against her better judgment, May reached for it and unfolded it. She jerked back when she saw the light was coming from a stamp at the bottom, of a pair of glowing red eyes. Written in dim letters above it were these words:

> *Hidey girl and scaredy cat,*
>
> *If you are reading this, you have come back to the Ever After. And that was a mistake, but it is not unexpected. I am looking for you. We are both singular sorts of spirits, and there is no way we can avoid one another. Remember, little speck. You will find me, or I will find you.*

There was no signature. Only the red eyes, which May knew were the eyes of Evil Bo Cleevil.

She looked around the room again. How long ago had this note been put here? Days, weeks, a year? What had happened to Pumpkin and Arista? Had the dark spirits taken them? Had Cleevil? She feared the worst. If she had been here, would she have been able to protect them? She pulled out one silver arrow from her pack and stared at it, gleaming, perfectly smooth.

She stood and with a heavy heart drifted into the spare room and sank into bed. She curled up with the arrow beside her and watched it shining in the dark, wondering. Finally, she lay back and drifted into a fitful sleep. Somber Kitty curled around her head like a pair of earmuffs, watching the door the long night through.

Whe May woke the following morning, her eyes were on the exact same spot she'd closed them on the night before: the tiny chandelier just above her head. She squinted for a moment, trying to make out what she was seeing.

She sat straight up. She stood up and squinted. There was something written in the dust that clung to the chandelier. It took her a moment to make the letters out, they were so smudged.

POD

"Meow," Somber Kitty said, sniffing the air.

There was no telling how long the message had been there. Had it been before the residents of Belle Morte had disappeared, or after? Did it mean what she thought it could mean? May looked at Somber Kitty, then leaped off the bed and hurried into Arista's study. She unrolled the map of the Ever After again.

There. May jabbed her finger at the spot on the map. Pit of Despair Amusement Park. It was in the west, south of the city of Ether and west of New Egypt. To get there, they would need to take the great road called the Trans-Realm Floatway, which ran along the Dead Sea, and then hooked west under the city of Ether.

There were a million reasons why it might turn out to be a dead end. Maybe "Pit of Despair" was not what the letters meant. Maybe the Pit of Despair was no longer standing.

But it would give her something to work toward until she had more direction. Until the Lady contacted her and told her what she needed to do next. Somewhere along the way, the Lady's help would surely find her.

She folded the map into a pocket inside her shroud, tucked Somber Kitty under her arm, and hurried out the front door.

Back in town, May ducked from building to building. Clutching her arrows tight, and hoping she'd have the courage to use them if she needed to, she scurried back into the Moldy Page and tucked Kitty safely onto one of the shelves, crawling about to find a Goblin-Ghoulish-Zombie to English dictionary and snatch a handful of gold coins from the register, which she didn't think the spirits of Belle Morte would miss any time soon.

She laid Kitty in the bicycle basket, covering him with an old, moldy blanket. And they took off, pedaling north.

Chapter Seven

Like a Ghost

The southern bluffs of the Ever After rose to overlook the dark, oily Dead Sea, which stretched off into the horizon as far as the eye could see. May and Kitty wove along the Trans-Realm Floatway, which hugged its outermost curves, May carefully steering the bike, her brows knitted in concentration, for fear that they would tumble over the side and fall into the dark waters below. Even though they could float with their shrouds on, it was very different from flying, and if they wandered off the edge, they would drop like stones into the sea. And any souls touched by even a drop of Dead Sea water would immediately be transported to dungeons in the dark realm far below its surface.

Kitty sat piggyback, his claws clutching the fabric of May's shroud, as they wove through towns perched on the cliffs— retirement communities like Shrouded Shores and Restful Recluses advertising skull bowling in the withered front lawns, budget resorts full of cozy graves such as Seaside Sarcophagi, and ritzy beachfront communities full of decrepit, crumbling mausoleums with million-dollar views of the dismal black sea. All were deserted.

Occasionally they had to stop so May could squint at the map, knowing the Floatway would bring them close to Nine Knaves Grotto, which, of course, was nowhere on the map. The grotto was a secret town full of pirates, bandits, bank robbers, and the like, where May had spent a night with its wild inhabitants and made a dangerous partnership with a shady knave named John the Jibber. Lucius had dwelled very close to there once, hiding with several other boys in the depths of the catacomb cliffs. Maybe he had come back. It seemed like it must be close.

She climbed off her bike and looked over the side of the cliff, the wind blowing back her long hair in thick black tangles, scanning the area below in either direction—the long, empty beach, the places where the sea oozed against the rocks. Her heart sped up when she spotted the tiniest path, winding down the cliffside.

With Kitty at her heels she wound down the path, until she was at a gaping hole that sat, like a cavity, in the side of the cliff. She hesitated, looking over her shoulder, then up at the sky. This was the realm of the luminous boys, and they were known to be mischievous. Sometimes too mischievous. The first time May had encountered them, she had ended up locked in a birdcage. She didn't want that to happen twice.

Still hovering uncertainly, she noticed something moving in the sky far over the ocean. It looked like black specks of oil at first, as if the water of the Dead Sea had escaped into the air. And then she could make out the separate, man-like figures. Instinctively, she stepped just inside the cool darkness of the cave, reaching out to pull Kitty in too. They waited in silence for a long time. Curiously, May noticed that she couldn't hear the sound of her own breath. A chill crept from the tips of her toes back through her heels and up to the roots of her hair.

Above, the creatures got closer. They were indeed men—capes hung from their backs like wings, their faces pale, their hair black and glinting. May knew she should retreat farther into the cave, but she couldn't look away—soon they were close enough that she could just make out their faces, and then fangs that poked out from their closed lips. *Vampires!* And then they were directly overhead, and their eyes were swiveling in her direction. At the last moment, May ducked back into the dark. Nothing happened for several seconds.

When she looked out moments later, they were gone. She waited a few more seconds and then stepped out from the over-hang of the cave, peering into the sky all around, and then down at the sea below. A few planks floated on the surface of the water. One of them looked like a sign. May squinted at it: N.K.G. SCHOOL OF THIEVERY AND PICKPOCKETING.

"They destroyed it."

May whipped around. A glowing boy stood in the cave open-ing. He had red, spiky hair, big ears, freckles, and the unmis-takable white glow of a luminous boy. May recovered herself enough to back up a couple of steps.

"A few years ago," the boy continued, "right after that liv-ing girl took Lucius away. We ventured out the next day, look-ing for him, and there the ghouls were in the Grotto, tearing it down."

May knew the luminous boys rarely ventured out of the

Catacombs at all. They were too fearful of what awaited them outside. She cleared her throat, feeling suddenly shy. "Ahem. Is . . . is Lucius here now?"

The boy looked her up and down. "Who wants to know?" he growled, obviously trying to sound tough.

"I'm the girl you were talking about. May Bird. I really need to find Lucius."

"Noooo." The boy shook his head thoughtfully. "No, it wasn't you. This girl was small, and alive."

"I've grown," May said. "But I'm still that living girl."

A mischievous grin spread across the boy's freckled face. "Well, don't you think you're tricky." He thrust out his skinny chest proudly. "I know a living girl when I see one." He gestured to her translucent, ghostlike body. "And *you* are not one. You're a specter, all right."

"Oh," May breathed, realizing the problem. "This is just my death shroud." She reached to pull back her shroud, throwing it over her shoulders. "See?"

He looked her up and down, unimpressed, and crossed his arms. "Do I look like I died yesterday?"

May stared at him for a moment, boggled, and then glanced down at herself. When she saw her own body, she gasped. Nothing had changed. She still floated. She still glowed, translucent, like a ghost.

She threw the shroud back farther, violently. Then, as if it were full of roaches or spiders, she frantically worked on the knot at her neck to untie it, yanking it off her shoulders and dropping it to the ground. She couldn't make sense of what she was seeing. She turned to Somber Kitty and pulled off his shroud. He, too, still hovered, ghosty. She looked at the boy, as if he could help her make sense of it all. Her head was spinning. But he was looking up at the sky, at where the vampires had passed overhead. "They're always in the sky, looking for her," the boy whispered.

"Who are *they*?" May demanded, her head all jumbled, her heart beating lopsidedly as a one-man band.

The boy looked at her for a moment, and then his gaze darted to something behind her shoulders, and his eyes widened. In a moment he was a flash of light, zipping off into the depths of the cave. The light of him lingered for a moment longer in the deep shadows of the tunnel and then disappeared, leaving the Catacombs completely black.

May felt a hard poke jab into her back.

"Well, ain't it fancy meeting you here?" a gravelly voice said behind her.

Instinctively May reached for her arrows, but the thing in her back jabbed harder, making her stumble forward. "Eh-eh-eh. Hands up. Turn around real slow like, or yer likely to get all wet."

May scanned the ground for Kitty, but he'd disappeared. She raised her hands into the air and swiveled slowly, as a rough hand reached out and slid her bow over her head.

Three familiar faces greeted her, Somber Kitty squirming in the arms of the figure to the left. May had seen them all before, when Nine Knaves Grotto was still standing. The specter in the center had a scraggly beard, dimpled chubby cheeks, a patch over one eye, and he held a water gun full of Dead Sea water in his left hand.

"Allow me to introduce myself," he said, reaching out his grimy free hand. "I'm Peg Leg Petey." He squinted. "Ye've grown like a vine. But it's you all right."

He looked May up and down, then smiled to reveal seven golden teeth in an otherwise empty mouth. He reached one hand around her wrist firmly. With the other he pulled a length of rope from his pocket. He winked at her and grinned more widely. "And you look like a million bucks."

Chapter Eight

The Last of the Knaves

"T was only a small group of us what made it out, thanks to our smarts," Petey was saying, plucking a hair from his scraggly beard and using it to floss his golden teeth. "A knave's always got to have an escape route."

Petey, sitting in the driver's seat of the car, which was painted the exact color of the desert so that it was almost impossible to spot from more than a few feet away, wore a striped pirate shirt that accentuated his bulging belly. One wooden leg protruded from his baggy trousers. In the back with her wrists tied together, May was flanked on one side by a chunky woman with round, bluish cheeks who, May knew, went by the name of Guillotined Gwenneth. She had a purple gash along her neck where she had clearly been beheaded, and her brown eyes twinkled with malicious mirth as she stared at May. Somber Kitty, whom Gwenneth held on her lap tightly, looked to be smothering in her copious bosom. On May's right sat a beanpole of a man in a black-and-white-striped prison suit, who had introduced himself as Skinny Skippy and now sat fiddling nervously with her quiver of arrows, licking his dry lips and rocking back and forth slightly.

It had been a long time since May had felt the coldness of a spirit's touch. But as they lurched along beyond the cliffs and back into the desert, she stared out the window, numb to the danger that came with sitting in a car full of knaves. She kept running over events in her mind at top speed. Falling off the roof. The lake suddenly appearing. The open doorway. It was all too clear to ignore.

They were dead. Dead. Dead. As doornails.

May had pictured herself as being a lot of things when she grew up, but none of them included being a spirit drifting around the afterlife in a bathing suit and pajama bottoms. *Nevers* crowded her mind like beetles, one piling on top of the next, each one a fresh shock. She would never grow an inch taller, never have a boyfriend, never go to high school, never visit the real Egypt, never see White Moss Manor again. But most of all, more hurtful than any *never* that popped into her head, May thought of those nights her mom had reached for her in the middle of the night, just to make sure she was there.

She stared down at her translucent body, trying to picture an eternity floating, filmy, and gray. She looked over at Somber Kitty, who was staring at her quizzically, his giant translucent ears tilted toward her like satellites. Did *he* know they were dead? He looked very melancholy, but after all, that *was* his favorite expression, and they *were* being kidnapped by knaves. May turned to the window again, tears gathering in her eyes.

Petey, who happened to be looking back over his shoulder just then, frowned. "There, there, lassie, don't try to hold it back," he said, his voice sounding all choked up. "Ain't no shame in it. Sometimes I cry too, ye know."

"Every time ye so much as stub yer toe, or see a wee poltergeist trapped at the zoo!" Gwenneth chortled. Skinny Skippy laughed through his nose, nodding his head up and down.

Petey frowned deeper and turned back to driving.

"The ghouls came right after you left, lassie," Skinny Skippy said, grinning. "You and the Jibber and your friends. That bright white boyfriend o' yours and that pathetic house ghost, Squashie."

May was barely listening. She cast a glance at Skippy, who licked his smiling lips, worms crawling out of the holes in his shirt. "He's not my boyfriend," she muttered.

"Say." Petey looked into the cracked rearview mirror. "What happened to you anyway? How'd ye die? Asphyxiation? Drowning?" May kept her mouth shut. She didn't know how she continued to exist right then. She felt like she should disintegrate completely, so empty did she feel.

"Well, the Ever After's changed a great deal since we last had the pleasure of your comp'ny," he went on. Gwenneth and Skippy rolled their eyes at each other at the words "pleasure of your company," and Gwenneth pantomimed Petey's fine manners. She nodded toward the front passenger seat, drawing May's attention to a book that lay there: *How to Win Friends, Influence Specters, Have Good Manners, and Find Buried Treasure* by Duke Bluebeard, Esquire. Petey, not noticing, continued. "All our friends—gone, lassie. And knaves bein' the best souls at hidin' themselves and bein' sneaky." He sighed. "Ah well, I'd say the others what dwelled in the Grotto have crossed the bridge by now. I'd say lots of spirits all over the realm have, since Cleevil took over." He sniffed. "Poor things."

"Bridge . . ." May murmured, hardly caring that she didn't know what he was talking about.

Gwenneth let out a derisive grunt. "You know about the Bridge of Souls?" she asked, with a malicious grin, clearly dying to share.

May shook her head numbly.

Gwenneth and Skinny Skippy gave each other a meaningful look.

"Best not talk about that, ye two," Petey said warningly over his shoulder, then let out a huge, smelly burp. Somber Kitty tucked his nose against Gwenneth's bosom. "Some folks say it sneaks up on you if you talk about it too much." Gwenneth's eyes widened with fear, as if realizing he had a point. And then she seemed to have a new thought.

"Ay." She sighed. "I do feel sorry fer ye, lassie, being newly dead's no picnic. Bit of a shock, it is." She hesitated, scratching at the mark around her neck from where she'd been beheaded. "And ye know, it makes me a sight sorry about trying to get ye wet all those years ago, with that nasty seawater capsule," she said, reaching out a hand to shake. "Let's make up."

"There's one in your hand right now," May said flatly, staring down at the black capsule tucked between Gwenneth's fingers, ready to pop.

Gwenneth feigned surprise. "Ay, so there is!" she said, sheepishly slipping the capsule back into her pocket and showing May her big, black-toothed smile.

"Bet people on Earth are a bit on edge these days, eh?" Petey said, cheerfully making conversation. May barely heard him, wondering what her funeral would be like. Would somebody be there to hold her mom's hand? What kind of music would they play?

Up ahead, the City of Ether came into view, and they all fell silent, leaning forward breathlessly. Even for spirits who saw it every day, the city was breathtaking: its spiky rooftops, the great churches that soared above its walls, and the enormous gray spire of the Eternal Edifice, which rose so high into the air that its roof couldn't be seen—it merely disappeared into the sky.

The city was surrounded by an enormous cemetery filled with hundreds of thousands of graves for nightly haunting duties.

Ether itself was still alight, eerie glows coming from the windows. But even from this far away, May could see that the great phantoms that once guarded its four gates were gone.

"Bo Cleevil called the sniffing phantoms home last year sometime," Gwenneth said, following her eyes. "'Tweren't necessary anymore. Now he's just got the vampires roaming the skies."

May could just make out a giant structure up ahead, several stories tall, just outside the city gate. That was new. It was a billboard of sorts, with a dark shadowy figure on it, all in black, moving back and forth with decisive, quick movements. The way it moved, powerful and menacing, reminded her of Bo Cleevil. She imagined she could make out his long trench coat, his beaten hat, his slick-as-a-snake movements. But as they got closer, she realized it was a different shape—similar, but smaller, thinner, more graceful.

As they drove closer and closer, another gut-pounding thought occurred to her: If she was dead, that meant the Lady hadn't sent for her. She hadn't brought her here. She might not even know that May was in the Ever After.

At that same moment, something about the tilt of the figure on the billboard up ahead made May's ears go red and itchy. If her heart had still been beating, it would have skipped. It couldn't be . . . but then, now that she saw it, there was no mistaking it. Things—which a moment ago seemed about as bad as they could get—got worse.

Looming ahead was a moving picture—several stories high—of a figure with her death shroud blowing behind her, a sinister look on her face, her black bathing suit sparkling. It was a ten-year-old May Bird, towering over Ether for all the world to see. Across the top was one word: WANTED, glowing in moving red letters. And along the bottom: A MILLION BUCKS FOR HER CAPTURE. COURTESY OF YOUR FAVORITE RULER, BO CLEEVIL.

May looked down at her tied hands and knew now why the knaves had taken her. She wriggled her wrists, but Skinny Skippy put his water gun to her side and gave her a look that said not to dare.

"We float from here," he said.

May had no choice but to drift out of the car behind the knaves as they made their slow progress up the ramp that led onto the wall of the city.

"Yep," Petey said, as much to himself as to May, looking around at the thousands of headstones behind them, then up at the Eternal Edifice, its impossibly high spire arching far above their heads. "Hard to believe Cleevil's finally got his hands on *The Book of the Dead*. They say that's what told him how to use the graves."

"What do you mean 'use the graves'?" May asked, a sudden fear taking hold of her, though she didn't know exactly why.

"Why," Petey said, looking surprised, "how to use other spirits' graves without getting lost. That's how he means to do it, ye know. What do ye think all the Cleevilvilles are for? For the dark spirits, of course. Thousands and thousands of 'em. Goblins, ghouls, vamps, whatnot." He nodded to himself. "Yep, I'd say they're just about ready to go."

"Go where?" May asked, her stomach turning sickly.

"Why, to go take over the land of the living, of course," he said, chewing on something. "Didn't ye know?" He motioned to the vast graveyard behind them, a giant version of the cemeteries that stood in every town in the Ever After, all full of doorways to the world below. He reached a finger into his mouth and pulled out a cockroach, but May hardly noticed. "Earth's the next to go."

Chapter Nine

Ghost City

May and her captors drifted up the main boulevard, tumbleweeds flying past them. The dusty streets of Ether, once filled with bustling merchants, hangmen, Victorian specters bustling off to haunting duties, shades in saris and silks, spirits hawking souvenirs from rusted carts, were empty. Tiny hovels, cottages, gaping mausoleums, intricate crumbling chapels lined the boulevards and crisscrossing alleys, but nothing more. Even the stone gargoyles that had once lined the tops of walls of the city were gone.

It was impossible, May thought. *Impossible*. The Ever After was full of ancient rules. And one of them was "Hopping graveys is for babies." Which meant, no spirits could use other spirits' graves to haunt the Earth.

"You're right to look scared, girly. They probably gonna turn ye ta nothin' when we hand ye over," Skinny Skippy said gleefully, misinterpreting her stricken expression.

They stopped at an empty bakery with crispy skull-shaped pastries in the window display, and cupcakes coated in thick white frosting made to look like brains, and tiny, intricate marzipan coffins. The knaves raided the shelves and stuffed their faces, grinning at one another with their rotten teeth. May stared at them, lost. From time to time, Kitty swiped his paw softly at her cheek, trying to wake her from her daze. But finding out she was dead, that she was also up for ransom, and that her entire planet was on the brink of being invaded by every ghoul, goblin, and zombie in existence was too much for her. Something inside her had crumpled up, checked out, so that even Somber Kitty's soft paw pads couldn't rouse her.

"Ay, that last skullcake's got me name on it," Skinny Skippy growled.

"And Santa's coming early this year," Petey shot back, grabbing the pastry and stuffing it into his mouth, then winking at Skippy, his cheeks bulging. That was all it took for Skippy, who hauled back and punched Petey in the face. Petey stumbled back and drew his water gun at the same time Skippy did. Somber Kitty, perched in May's arms, watched, fascinated, his head moving back and forth as if he were at a tennis match.

"'At's enough, boys," Gwenneth said, thrusting one smelly foot between them. Skippy acted quickly, pulling out his dagger and slicing it off.

"Yow!" she yelled, lunging after her foot, which landed a few feet away. "What'd ye go and do that for?" She picked up the foot, the toes wiggling. "As if I ain't got enough to carry and now I gotta be carryin' me own foot." She looked around, as if she might find something to tie the foot back on with, and then she sighed and tucked it under her arm.

They wove through the city slowly, Petey stopping them every time they reached a corner or an open doorway to make sure the coast was clear. "Still a few dark spirits running about," he said, "though most of 'em have moved on now that the city's deserted. . . ."

The knaves, seeming a little discomfited by May's utter silence, were trying to make conversation.

"Ye may wonder where we're takin' ye," Gwenneth prattled on. "There's a captive drop-off spot north of here, in West Stabby Eye, right next to the drop-off for Bad Will."

They were in a district called Glow-So, which, by the looks of it, was the high fashion capital of the realm. The street was lined with stores displaying filmy garments full of holes and coated in intricate, moldy, and spiderwebbed patterns. Some were covered in customized dark stains, others were simply worn-out and nubby. They wove through the neighborhoods of Little Groany, All Hags Haven, and Phantasm Phairway, Peg Leg Petey explaining that in the city's heyday, this was where you got the best hexes, and that was the hottest spot to buy phantasmic phootwear, and this was where you went to see the best new musicals. What was left behind by the city's inhabitants—bits of paper scrawled with glowing words and blood red ink, old wedding veils, top hats, blobs of ectoplasm—fluttered up and down the crisscrossing alleyways and avenues with the breeze.

And then they turned a corner and suddenly it was before them—the Eternal Edifice.

The Edifice's great golden doors lay on the street, broken in pieces. Its windows were all missing. Ghouls had graffitied its walls with words such as "Hgggbbleeeee" and "Argglbll ggubkllbbllll!"

"Argglbll ggubkllbbllll." Petey sighed. "Now that's a bit naughty."

Even the knaves were awed by the hollowed remains of the Edifice.

Listlessly May drifted toward it, reaching out her bound hands, peering up its once-gleaming white walls, now dull and grimy. And then she was close enough to see that, underneath the graffiti and the grime, the words of wishes—which she had seen once before—were still etched across the building's surface. Her eyes fell to the ground, where a shard of stained glass lay beneath her. Something poked out from underneath it—a piece of paper, fluttering at her in the breeze. She stared at it for a moment. And suddenly, the fog in May's head lifted.

FINAL PERFORMANCE IN THE EVER AFTER! ONE NIGHT ONLY!

The photo was of Pumpkin, dressed in a turban. He was standing near a pile of fake jewels, moving his mouth as if he were singing. May held the paper close to her ear. She could hear the faint but unmistakable sound of Pumpkin's magnificent voice. She pulled back and looked again. He winked, but there was a sadness to his wink. A momentary wistful frown crossed his big, crooked mouth.

May felt like a person waking up from a dream. She had to pull herself—as flimsy and translucent as she might be—together.

She chewed a nail and stared at the picture, Pumpkin waving his jewels and treasure. She felt a tug at her wrists.

"All right, missy," Skippy said, sneering and licking his lips. "Let's get a move on."

Quickly May grabbed the paper and stuffed it into her pocket. She shot Somber Kitty a look. Kitty, tight in Gwenneth's arms and his usual discreet self, didn't say anything.

"Hey, you know," May said thoughtfully, a few minutes later, as they were making their way down an empty boulevard in the direction of the northern gate, "you really shouldn't turn me in."

Gwenneth let out a hardy laugh. "Oh yeah? Why's that?"

May thought of Pumpkin's picture, which had reminded her of something else. "Because I know where you can find something that's worth much more than a million bucks."

Skinny Skippy laughed and Gwenneth yawned, clearly disbelieving. But Peg Leg Petey looked intrigued and rubbed his scraggly chin. "Oh yeah? And what's that?"

"Well if you're not interested in the treasure of the Queen of Sheeba . . ."

The knaves stood staring for a moment. Greed twinkled in Petey's eye. It glistened in a drop of drool that rolled from Skippy's mouth. It glinted off Gwenneth's three gold teeth.

"She lies," Skippy said.

May sighed. "Okay. Whatever . . ."

Suddenly May was being swept into Skippy's arms, a water gun pointed at her chin. "Now Skippy, be nice, lad," Petey said, reaching out for him and giving May an apologetic look with his one exposed eyeball, but Skippy jerked May backward another step.

"Explain yerself, lassie—yyyOW!"

Skippy leaped into the air, waving his gun toward the

ground, where Somber Kitty had landed, a piece of fabric dangling from his mouth. "He bit me bum!" Skippy yelped.

"Ay, to the devil with the both of ye," Gwenneth cried, snatching the gun out of Skippy's hands. "You"—she waved the gun at Skippy—"with yer skinny little munchkin legs, and you"—she waved the gun at Petey. She pointed the gun at May herself, waving it every now and then at Somber Kitty, too. "Now, explain yerself, girly."

May cleared her throat. "Remember John the Jibber came with me to find it?" It was true. She and John the Jibber had joined forces to reach the top of the Eternal Edifice so they could read the all-knowing *Book of the Dead*. May had wanted to find out if the book could tell her the way back to West Virginia. And John had wanted it to tell him where the treasure was. All they'd discovered, though, was the passage under May's name that read *Known far and wide as the girl who destroyed Evil Bo Cleevil's reign of terror*.

"Yeah," Gwenneth said, nodding at the other two. "I remember something about that."

"And ye're saying ye found it?" Petey asked, squinting at her.

May nodded. She wasn't used to lying, and she felt a guilty blush creeping up her face. She could feel her ears turning red.

"So if the Jibber were here," Petey went on, "he'd say ye're telling the truth, and not to send you seven leagues under?"

May's throat went dry and icy. "Yes," she said evenly.

Petey hesitated. "Well he *is* here."

May went cold. It was impossible. Wasn't it? She peered around, as if John the Jibber might be standing right behind her.

There was an uncomfortable silence in which Gwenneth cleared her throat and exchanged a questioning glance with Skippy. And then Petey reached deep into his pocket and pulled out a rubber band. "I got this via Pony Express, from the City of Ether, a few weeks after ye two left."

"What is it?" May asked.

Petey looked at her as if the answer were obvious. "Why, it's John the Jibber. They turned him into a rubber band."

The other knaves' mouths dropped open.

May stared at the rubber band, speechless.

"You told us that was only yer *lucky* rubber band," Skinny Skippy said.

"What're ye doin carryin' around John the Jibber with ye everywhere ye go?" Gwenneth added derisively.

May had to look down at her feet and bite her lip to keep from laughing. Clearly Petey believed the newspaper stories that said Jibber had been reincarnerated on his last trip to Ether. Reincarneration was what happened when you got dropped into a reincarnerator. You got changed into something else.

"'Tis me lucky rubber band too," Petey said, defending himself, but looking sheepish. He gazed down at the rubber band. "So what do ye say, Jibber? Does the girl lie?"

To no one's surprise but Petey's, the rubber band didn't answer.

He gave it a good shake, then his lips started to tremble. He rubbed his scraggly beard thoughtfully. "No worries," he said, smiling broadly, but the smile disappeared as he pulled the rubber band close to his lips and whispered, "Johnny, me boy, are ye mad at me?"

"You know," May said, "you have nothing to lose. If I take you to the treasure, you can let me go. If there's no treasure, you can still turn me in."

Petey swiped a tear from his eye and sniffed. "He's always giving me the silent treatment," he said. Then he looked around, embarrassed, made a big show of hardened carelessness, and dropped the rubber band on the ground. "And where is the treasure, then?"

"It's close." *Right near the Pit of Despair Amusement Park,* May thought.

She stared at him, waiting for his answer. They just needed to head in that direction, so she could have some time to think. And then . . . and then she didn't know. Hopefully, since there were only three of them, she and Kitty could throw them off. They had fought worse.

Skinny Skippy waved his water gun at her. "Well, let's go then, lassie."

As they moved on, she looked over her shoulder. Behind them, thinking no one was watching, Petey scooped up the rubber band and tucked it into his pocket, with all the love and care of a jeweler for his finest diamond.

Chapter Ten

Vampires!

"Yo ho, yo hee, I died upon the sea
Now I seen the light, it's clear and bright
There be no more thieving for me
And if you believe I'm telling you right
I got another one for thee."

The knaves seemed to have no dearth of songs about death and thieving and lying. They had already sung "When I Get My Hands on Your Booty," and this was the seventeenth verse of "Still Knavey After All These Years."

They had traveled out through the western gate of Ether, past a deserted village called New Venice, built on canals stretching off the Styx Streamway, and now they were moving southwest along a great, empty road full of potholes and lined with glowing old motels like the Forever Night Inn and the Sleepy Hollow, all deserted. Somber Kitty kept pace, one of his tiny ankles now tied to one of May's, so they looked like they were running a three-legged race.

By the blue campfire that night, May and Somber Kitty sat cuddling by the fire as the knaves hooted and hollered and enjoyed themselves. May was too distraught to notice. She was imagining a world full of dark spirits. She was imagining Briery Swamp full of ghouls.

May pulled out her picture of Pumpkin and looked at it. Somber Kitty patted his paw against Pumpkin's face affectionately. Was he okay?

Why hadn't she stayed and fought when she'd had the chance? Now everything was worse than she had ever imagined.

May thought of her friends—Beatrice, Lucius, Captain Fabbio, Pumpkin. If she got them back, she wouldn't let them down again, that much she was sure of. This time she would do it right.

She looked down at Kitty, making muffins on her knees. A thought flashed at her. She wiggled her hands so that her ropes slid under his claws. It was worth a try.

Somber Kitty gave her a keen look, and set to work making muffins.

May felt a shadow behind her and started, turning to see Skinny Skippy staring over her shoulder. She moved closer to the fire, pulling her hands to her stomach.

"Petey . . . ," she ventured after a moment, seeing that the knave was in an especially thoughtful mood, rubbing his rubber band gently against his cheek. "Is it true, about the dark spirits taking over the Earth?"

"Ay and sure it is, lassie. Cleevil's got it all figured out. Gotten so powerful he's trumped all the old rules, he has. Using *The Book of the Dead* to tell him how to get around things, I s'pose. And hardly any spirits left to go against him."

"Do you know what he does with all the spirits, once he takes them away?"

"Well, lassie," Petey said. "Nobody knows, really. The dark spirits come in and out—ghouls, goblins, mummies, the vamps, taking in prisoners and coming out empty-handed again. Once they're taken beyond the Platte of Despair, nobody ever hears from 'em again. I'll tell you one thing," he went on. "They say his castle's like a maze inside, workers always building rooms and such to confuse anyone who tries to get in, keeps getting taller and taller, with Cleevil tucked away at the very top so nobody can reach him. A bit paranoid, he is."

Gwenneth laughed. "And where'd ye hear all this, Petey? From the birdie what lives in yer backside?"

Petey straightened up defensively. "I hear things. Hm," he said, gazing across the featureless plains, "rock, sand, more rocks, yep, this is the spot. . . ."

He gave a whistle. "Ye, see, lassie," Petey said, avoiding her eyes. "We're gonna use yer ransom money to build us a new grotto."

Suddenly several rocks began to shake and roll as they were pushed aside, and knaves drifted out from pits they had dug underneath them. Three swarthy pirates with daggers, a gang of nasty-looking numbers wearing black-and-white-striped prison suits, and a gaggle of bandits with handkerchiefs over their mouths. It was a knave reunion.

In two seconds flat, the numbers of May and Kitty's captors grew from three to twenty-three. And they went from being merely trapped to being surrounded.

On their second day of traveling, Somber Kitty managed to get May's ropes unraveled. And the knaves began to get restless.

A sign came into view up ahead. It was big and silver, stretching in an arch across the desert. It read ALMOST THERE AT THE PIT OF DESPAIR! An hour after that they came to another: 100,000 SOUVENIRS FOR SALE! THE PIT OF DESPAIR! And still later, another: THREE TACO STANDS! THE PIT OF DESPAIR!

Finally, up ahead a giant square billboard appeared, with a huge red arrow pointing straight down and above it the words YOU'VE ARRIVED! THIS WAY FOR THE PIT OF DESPAIR AMUSEMENT PARK!

"Pumpkin," May whispered. She kept her hands down, pretending they were still tied. She felt restless and nervous, and she still had no plan. Skippy had floated up beside her, for several minutes just drifting along, making her feel uncomfortable.

"They say he begged and begged, yer friend."

May turned toward him. "What?"

"They say he begged to be set free. It was in all the newspapers. There was a whole crowd of people watching, of course. Being how famous he was and all. But they took him anyway."

"Who?"

He nodded at May's pocket, where she had tucked her picture of Pumpkin.

May squinted at him, her stomach aching. "I don't know what you're talking about."

Skippy stared at her in shock. "What! Yer best friend and ye didn't even know!" He laughed incredulously. "But every soul in the Ever After heard about it. It was in all the papers. There were holo-pics and everything. He was trying to sneak off, like, through the city, headed in this very direction. They say Cleevil himself got him. Turned him into nothing on the spot."

Every word he spoke throbbed in May's ears. She crossed

her arms to keep them from shaking. She shook her head, her throat suddenly very sore. "I don't believe you."

"Here." He dug through the sack that hung over his shoulder and pulled out a ratty old newspaper. "I kept a copy, a souvenir, like. Everybody did, what with him being so famous and all."

He handed May the paper. On the front was a photo of nothing in between two ghouls. REALM'S MOST BELOVED SINGER TURNED INTO NOTHING ON THE SPOT.

May let out a small cry.

"Ah, crying, eh? No use."

May swiped a frantic tear from her eye.

"Well, too late now anyway, idn't it?"

"Let the girl be." Peg Leg Petey had appeared beside them, pulling out a wet, gooey hanky and stuffing it into May's hand. May, in shock, only let the hanky dangle limply in her hand.

Skinny Skippy whipped a water gun out of his pocket. "Lay off, hey, Petey? I'm tired of waiting around." He turned his water gun on May. "I'm getting the feeling you don't know where any treasure is, lass."

He tightened his finger on the trigger. In an instant Peg Leg Petey had leaped in front of her, pulling out his own water gun. "Ye'll not touch a hair on her little head," he growled.

Skippy laughed. "Well then, so long, Petey. . . ."

Screeeeeeeeeeeeeeeeeeeeeeech!

All the knaves jumped, turning to look toward the horizon, where three black dots had appeared far in the distance. "Vampires," Petey whispered.

May swooped Kitty into her arms, her ropes flying off, and ran.

"She's getting away!" voices shouted behind her. She turned to see a gaggle of knaves running after her, pulling out their water guns. "Freeze right there!" But May kept going. Behind her she heard a screech, louder, and then felt a black shadow fall over her. She looked back just in time to see a pair of pale hands scooping Skinny Skippy into the air. He dropped May's bow and arrows onto the sand as he was whisked upward. The other knaves scattered as the vampires gave chase.

May bit her lip, gazed at her bow and arrows, and then doubled back, scooping them up. She stood up in time to see one of the vampires sailing down toward her. She looked back over her shoulder. She could run for it, but if the vampire saw her disappear into the Pit of Despair, it would surely follow.

She forced her feet to stand still.

As it loomed closer, she took aim—praying that she still remembered how—and fired, the force throwing her off balance. The vampire turned to stone midair and skidded past her. May gazed down at her bow, amazed at her own shot.

A screech in the distance was enough to set her on her feet again.

She took off in the direction of the Pit.

The sign was only a few feet before her now, and still May saw no indication of the entrance beneath it. She looked over her shoulder, saw the vampires turning in her direction, and slid across the sand like she was sliding into first base, slipping just under the lip of the sign as another vampire soared overhead and past her, unaware. And then she found she was still sliding, and then falling into the dark.

Chapter Eleven

The Pit of Despair

May and Kitty were sliding downward and around and around a dark basin, like water being flushed down a toilet. Then they were falling through the air. May wondered how badly it was going to hurt when she landed. They fell and fell, until the opening was only a pinprick of light. And then she hit something and bounced, and hit it, and bounced again. She couldn't see what it was because it was pitch-black all around her, but it felt like a trampoline. Eventually the bounces became smaller and smaller until she was lying on her face on mesh netting. Kitty flopped across her head. May rolled over and rolled off, landing with a *thunk* on the ground.

She stood and looked around. Everything was black but for a rectangular booth up ahead, lit from within by an eerie blue light. A figure stood inside the booth, also glowing with blue light, very still. She had on a moth-eaten cardigan sweater with a white collared shirt underneath. Her short hair was curled and frosted, and she wore glasses.

Warily, May drifted close enough to see that she wore a name tag: Edith. She was looking not at May, but off into the darkness to her right, as if she were bored.

"Uh." May hesitated, then cleared her throat. "Um, excuse me." Slowly, as if on a wheel, the woman turned toward her. She was missing one eye, and a worm crawled out of the hole where her missing eye had been. She said nothing, apparently waiting for May to speak.

May curled her fingers together, trying to buck up her courage. She was still reeling from the news about Pumpkin. "I was hoping this was the Pit of Despair Amusement Park?"

Slowly, as if it took all the effort in the world, the woman looked down at a roll of tickets sitting on the counter.

"Oh," May warbled, digging in her pockets. "Oh, how much?"

The woman only stared at her blankly.

May remembered the money she'd picked up in Belle Morte and pulled it out of her pocket. She pushed it across, hoping it was enough.

The woman stared at it for a moment. Then her crumbling, withered hands slowly ripped one of the tickets from the wheel and pushed it back at her through the slot.

"Thank you." May looked around at the darkness, then back at the woman questioningly. The woman let out a long sigh, and then turned in the direction she had been looking before.

Now that May looked harder, she could just make out what looked like a black velvet curtain there. She gulped, she and Kitty exchanged a glance, and they walked in that direction. The curtain opened slowly before them, but nothing was on the other side but darkness. She stepped inside and let the curtain fall shut behind her.

Far, far above—maybe twenty stories over her head—a red

light began to flash. A moment later a deafening buzzer went off all around them, shaking the ground beneath their feet. There were loud clickings and rumblings high up in the air, and in the red glow May could now see she was indeed in an enormous pit, lined with hundreds of tiers going up farther than the eye could see. Along the tiers were doors, and each door was opening. May started to back up, but suddenly she was being lifted from underneath and she fell down, into a floating wooden coffin. Grabbing Kitty, she tried to scramble out, but in a moment they were too high to leap.

Figures began to emerge from the doors, and it took a moment to see that they were mechanical, made of metal, moving like the animatronic Santa Clauses Bridey McDrummy kept on her lawn in Hog Wallow. There were thousands of them—spirits dressed like undertakers and women with hair full of cobwebs, white faces, and darkly circled eyes. They floated off their tiers, hung by gossamer strings from an unseen ceiling, and spun all over the place, executing languid flips and circles in the air, all around May, singing in haunting, mournful voices:

> *When things are just too good*
> *or you're missing a good scare,*
> *we'll set your knees to knockin'*
> *deep in the Pit of Despair.*
>
> *If you're up for feeling down*
> *Or you want to raise your hair,*
> *look no farther than the realm's top thrills*
> *deep in the Pit of Despair.*

Come inside, forget your cares
It's worse in here than what's out there.
Plus we've got funnel cakes to spare
deep in the Pit of Despair.

The coffin lifted them higher and higher, and in another moment it was like every bit of electricity in the universe zapped into life all around them, lighting up the immense darkness and revealing a great amusement park beneath them. It was enormous, dazzling, and dark—glowing with eerie purple, green, and blue lights.

The coffin began to move swiftly downward, into the thick of the scene before them, zipping along above a candlelit cobblestone pathway that wound its way through the park. Mechanical spirits, still singing, circled the coffin, holding glowing signs that said THE GRAND TOUR.

Rides zoomed and soared on either side of them. Giant slides, sprinkled here and there, reached up so high May couldn't see where they began. They passed a gaping cave to the left, a crooked sign dangling above it glowing with the words TUNNEL OF HORROR. To the right was a huge house of decayed splendor, its front terrace sagging into the ground, its shutters dangling from the windows or lying on the floor, and screams of terror issuing from inside. A sign by the railing read MURDEROUS MANSION. They drifted past NIGHT ON BANSHEE MOUNTAIN, a mountain that arched crookedly overhead, fire shooting from crevices near the top, and then past HOUSE OF VAMPIRES, the entrance a vampire's mouth standing wide open. There were waterfalls of what smelled like Slurpy Soda, rusty silver stands selling Putrid Pops and skullcakes in a rainbow of colors ranging from blood red to rot brown, and countless shops bursting with souvenirs—stuffed mummies, chainsaws, shackles imprinted with PIT OF DESPAIR in bright letters.

But though all the rides were in motion and the snack bars were brimming with goodies, there wasn't a spirit in sight. It was completely empty.

May scanned the ground for a glimpse of a single soul. The cobblestone way beneath them branched into other pathways that led to the rides, and here and there the ground was interrupted with pits marked with arrows pointing downward and signs such as THIS WAY FOR AN UNFORTUNATE SURPRISE or COFFIN CANDY DOWN HERE IF YOU DARE. They crossed over a metal mummy-filled swamp, past a collection of rockets promising excursions to view nearby stars, a boat basin at the side of the Styx Streamway that, May assumed, must be for all the visitors who would normally be arriving from all over the realm. But there was no one.

Up ahead May could see the black curtain where she'd entered, and she realized they had been going in a big circle. The spirits in the air began to slow down their dancing and flipping, singing slower and slower, their voices beginning to wane. The coffin slowed to a stop, and the spirits floated back into the doorways above, waving mournfully before the doors slid shut. May and Somber Kitty looked around, then May scooped the cat into her arms and climbed out of the coffin.

As soon as she landed, a map floated into her hands, seemingly from nowhere, showing the different rides, each lit a different eerie color. *What next?* it asked. May stared. "I don't know," she muttered out loud.

Perhaps the Murderous Mansion? it suggested.

May shook her head. If she wasn't here for Pumpkin, why was she here? Taking a deep breath to keep her tears at bay, she drifted onto one of the cobblestone pathways, finding herself in a grove of dead, forbidding trees whose limbs seemed to reach out as if to grab them. Maybe there were others. Maybe the knaves had been lying. She wasn't ready to let herself crumble yet.

"If anyone's here," May muttered, gazing around, "where are they hiding?" Aside from the whir of the rides and the flash of the lights, nothing moved or made a sound. May sighed, looking down at her map again.

The Tunnel of Horror had begun to flash.

May climbed into the waiting boat at the mouth of the Tunnel of Horror and put Kitty beside her on the bench. The water underneath them was dark, obscuring whatever might be lurking underneath. As soon as they were both sitting, the boat lurched into motion. May held on to Kitty tightly as they were swallowed by darkness, listening to the drips of the cave around them.

May's fingers scratched nervously behind Kitty's ears. He wriggled out of her grasp, his green eyes giving her an annoyed look in the dark.

They waited for what would jump out of the dark to scare them. A whispering began all around them, terrifying, low, and menacing. Out of the corner of May's eye, she caught a light to the right, and down an alley she saw a sign: HORRIFIC HAMBURGERS—FILL UP BEFORE YOU FREAK OUT. The vaguest sound of laughter issued from behind the door of the building. Was it a recording, or actual spirits? May wondered. The boat stopped momentarily. She hesitated a moment, while it lurched into motion again, and then she grabbed Kitty and hopped out.

The door to Horrific Hamburgers was heavy, and it opened with a creak as May pushed with all her strength. She nearly stumbled back when she saw the room full of spirits that waited on the other side. They were all sitting around at various tables and along a mahogany bar, watching holo-vision. There was a woman in a black suit holding the hand of a young brown-skinned girl in a pink party dress, and a couple in colorful clothes and beads sat hand-in-hand, though one hand was not connected to a body. A girl with long black hair, wearing a sari, nodded at her gravely. A few blobbish, misshapen ghosts with horns and big teeth and bulbous noses and blue lips stared at Somber Kitty and nudged each other, and then turned their attention back to the holo-vision.

The filmy bartender—who had a handlebar mustache above his blue lips and wore an apron and cuffs, grinned over at her.

"Pull up a stool, young miss. Have a Slurpy Soda." He gazed at Somber Kitty.

May floated up to the bar. The bartender poured her a glass of the slimy and putrid-smelling drink. She took it politely into her hands but couldn't bring herself to sip it. She had never thought to wonder what was in a Slurpy Soda, but it smelled like worm pee and moth breath.

"Where ya fleeing from?"

"Excuse me?" May asked. The bartender smiled at her sadly.

"Ether, northern regions, Seaside?"

"Fleeing?"

"Which Cleevilville did they turn your town into? Mine was seventy-three. All my friends . . ." He trailed off sadly, turning his attention to a glass mug, which he began to polish.

"So is this . . . a hideout?" May asked.

He looked at her askance, clearly surprised that she didn't already know. "One of the last in the realm, long as none of the dark spirits find us." He sighed, laying down the mug and picking up another one. "We're making the best of it." He glanced again at Somber Kitty, who'd wrapped himself around May's neck like a scarf. "We get all kinds. But it's not every day we see a cat spirit. They were the first to go, you know."

May knew. Cats had been the first animals banished from the Ever After, because the evil Black Shuck Dogs were deathly afraid of them. Now all the animals—even the Shuck Dogs— were gone . . . to no one knew where.

May took it in—the room full of misplaced spirits, hiding in the belly of the Tunnel of Terror. And they were the lucky ones. It made her want to cry. "Actually, I came here looking for my friend," May said, her throat starting to knot up. "But he . . ." May couldn't bring herself to say it. She cleared her throat. "He . . ."

Seeing the tears welling in her eyes, the bartender pulled a decayed, hole-riddled tissue from his vest pocket and handed it to her.

"Hey, you're that girl." May looked up. It was the girl with the sari who'd spoken. A few spirits looked from the holo-vision in her direction again, curious.

"Oh yeah," another one said. "It's that one who's supposed to save the world from certain doom."

"Who?"

"May Burg or something."

"Bird," May said. "May Bird."

"Oh yeah."

A few spirits eyed her curiously and then turned back to the holo-vision.

"No wonder there's no hope," someone muttered darkly, but May couldn't see who. She looked down at herself self-consciously—taller, but still as skinny as ever. She felt like apologizing for herself. She hadn't turned out to be much of a warrior.

"Don't mind them," the bartender said listlessly. "They're just depressed. It's because we know Cleevil'll find us here one day too. There's nowhere to hide anymore."

"But . . . why aren't you trying to do anything about it?" May asked. Someone, maybe the same someone as before, laughed. The bartender scowled in their general direction.

"May Bird, ha," a spirit muttered.

"Well, *The Book of the Dead*'s been wrong before," someone else added.

"It has?" May sputtered.

Several spirits laughed. "Sure! You don't think the future's set in stone, do you? It hasn't even *happened* yet," one explained.

The bartender interrupted. "Now, you were saying something about looking for someone. . . ."

May shook her head, still absorbing what the spirit had said about *The Book of the Dead*. Could it have been wrong? Was it possible? "It's just," she said dazedly, "I came here looking for my friend Pumpkin, but . . ."

It was as if May had shot an arrow through the middle of the room. Everyone looked over at once.

"Pumpkin? The singer?" the bartender asked.

May nodded, taken aback.

"You're friends with *the* Pumpkin?" the girl in the sari said.

May nodded again.

Now everyone in the bar was hopping out of their chairs, circling around her, reaching out to touch her and shake her hand.

"I'd love an autograph," someone said.

"You don't have a lock of his hair you're willing to sell by any chance, do you?"

"Sightings are very rare."

May was befuddled. "Sightings?"

A few spirits nodded. "It's a shame, but he likes his privacy."

"But . . . ," May said, her heart twisting sharply. "But I guess you haven't heard. He . . . he was turned into nothing."

Everyone paused, very shocked. And then a roar of laughter swept the room.

"Oh, he's good," someone said, nodding.

"Typical Pumpkin."

May, bewildered, swept Somber Kitty into her arms, nervous, wondering if these spirits were lunatics. "What do you mean?"

"Do you believe everything you read in the paper?" the girl in the pink party dress asked, grinning. "Pumpkin's always spreading rumors to put off his fans. A few months ago it was that he ran off with Mary Washington to Elysian Acres. Before that he was abducted by aliens."

"Ha, aliens," said one woman with a knife sticking out of her head. "Everyone knows aliens don't exist."

"Pumpkin lives!" someone shouted.

"You're all fooling yourselves," the bartender interrupted. "Pumpkin got turned into nothing. I saw the picture myself." The half of the spirits who hadn't spoken up seemed to agree, and they nodded.

May felt like she was being twisted into a million shapes—the hope she'd been beginning to feel plummeted again.

"It's all wishful thinking," one of the blobbish ghosts boomed. "Spirits'll make up anything because they want to believe it. I heard a rumor just the other day he's hidden himself in the karaoke lounge, over on the far side of this very park." Several spirits laughed.

The bartender smiled his sad smile. "'Course we don't dare venture out of the Tunnel of Terror. Never know when the ghouls might wander down here into the Pit."

But May, Kitty at her heels, was already pushing open the door.

Chapter Twelve

The White Knuckle Karaoke Lounge

LIVE MUSIC! REFRESHMENTS!

May stood and stared at the entrance to the White Knuckle Karaoke Lounge, which she had found using her map. It was perched on a slight rise, on a dark, empty hill at the far end of the park. She swallowed, then pushed her way through the double doors into a dimly lit hallway. It stretched into the darkness, framed records hanging on the walls, all spinning and giving off soft music in countless languages. Moments later she emerged into a smoky room. A handful of spirits sat in red-upholstered chairs facing a small black stage, one of them smoldering, as if he'd just been on fire.

The stage before them was lit by a single spotlight. And in the single spotlight, on a moldy red couch, facedown, lay a lanky figure singing into a microphone.

"*Alll byyyyy myyyyselllllf . . .*" The voice was mournful and painful to the ears, resembling the sound of a dying cow. "*Don't want to be dead by myself . . . anymore. . . .*"

May stood rooted to the spot. "Mew," Kitty whispered, breathlessly.

Hearing Kitty, the figure's head perked to the right, just slightly. It sat up, swiveling halfway. May rushed forward. At that moment she felt herself grabbed by the elbows and yanked backward. Two spirits in red velvet suits had jumped out of their seats and had her by either arm. Somber Kitty leaped to her side and sank his teeth deep into one of the spirits' ankles. He howled.

"Pumpkin!" May yelled, struggling.

The figure onstage turned all the way around now, still holding the microphone to its lips. The large, lopsided, pumpkin-shaped head, all white and pasty, the big black eyes, the crooked mouth, would have been terrifying to someone who didn't know the creature they belonged to. Pumpkin's yellow hair flopped as he looked at May in astonishment.

"Pumpkin, it's me!" May yelled.

For a moment, pure joy crossed Pumpkin's face, his crooked mouth widening into a ghastly smile. But the moment it did, it turned downward into an angry frown that he directed first at her, then at Kitty, then off into nowhere, as if he'd forgotten they were standing there. With a flick of his finger, he summoned the smoking ghost from where he had risen to the edge of the stage, and whispered something into his ear. The ghost nodded and straightened up, addressing May with thin blue lips under a thin black mustache.

"He says, 'Look what the cat dragged in.'"

May looked at Pumpkin, who crossed his arms and looked off backstage as if he were bored. He began plucking at the split ends of his yellow tuft of hair. May was speechless. She opened and closed her mouth a few times in Pumpkin's direction, and then in the direction of the smoldering ghost, and sputtered, "Who are you?"

The ghost, his mustache twitching, straightened his blackened necktie. "I'm Pumpkin's publicist. Avril."

"Your publicist?!" May yelled to Pumpkin, baffled. Pumpkin turned to Avril and whispered something, then crossed his arms again and looked away.

"Pumpkin has asked that you direct all questions to me."

"Pumpkin . . ." May groaned. "What? Why?"

Pumpkin seemed to consider whether to answer or not. And then he whispered something to Avril.

"He says in case you don't remember, you abandoned him to a life of loneliness and sorrow."

May's heart sank. She hung her head. "Tell him I'm sorry. But I'm back now."

Pumpkin sighed loudly, then whispered.

"He says he's almost been captured by ghouls lots of times and you weren't around to help."

May searched for some way to reply, to defend herself. "But he wanted me to go. He said he hoped I'd never come back."

Pumpkin seemed to consider this for a long moment, and then another whisper, and Avril turned to May. "He says he thought he meant it at the time, but he didn't."

May didn't know what to say to that. Pumpkin shot a glance at her, and his lopsided forehead wrinkled. He smoothed out the tuft on top of his head thoughtfully. And then he leaned over and whispered again.

"He says how does he know you won't leave him again?"

May bit her lip, hopeful. "I don't know. Pumpkin, I'll just do my best. I'll try my best to never let you down again."

Pumpkin looked interested now. He stared at her and mumbled something.

"He says you look different. He says you don't look like a little girl anymore."

Because she couldn't raise her hands, May shrugged her shoulders, helplessly. She suddenly felt tall and gangly and unwieldy, perched there on her coltish legs, her long black hair tangled. "I grew up," she said to Pumpkin apologetically, her voice creaking a little. "And, well." Her voice cracked. "I also . . . died."

Pumpkin gave a small jerk. A big tear formed at the ridge of his left eye and slowly dribbled down his cheek. He nodded to the two ghosts holding May's arms, and they let her go.

May hesitated for a moment. And then, swooping like a Dodo bird, Pumpkin sprang forward, flinging his long arms wide open. May made up the distance, and in a moment she was in his cold embrace, being hugged so tight she felt like she might shrink into nothing. Pumpkin pulled back and gazed at her, his smile huge, hugged her again, pulled back again. Then he let out a squeal as he scooped Somber Kitty into his arms.

"Mwah mwah mwah mwah mwah!" He covered Somber Kitty in kisses, and Somber Kitty pretended to be disgusted, though he obviously liked it. He licked Pumpkin's nose, and Pumpkin squeezed him tight.

Finally May pulled back and gave him a nervous, hopeful look. She was almost as tall as his chest now. "Pumpkin," she gushed, hardly able to catch her breath, "where are the others? Where's Bea, and Fabbio, and Lucius? What about Isabella and Arista?"

Pumpkin's smile descended, once again, into a deep frown.

He looked around at his publicist and bodyguards as if they were suddenly in the way. He sighed theatrically. "Where does a star go to get some privacy around here?" But the look he gave May was anything but theatrical. And it filled her heart with dread.

Chapter Thirteen

The Lorelei

"So the spirits are just hiding here waiting for the end of the Ever After?" May asked.

Pumpkin had led May across the amusement park, through a series of camouflaged doors hidden in the dead trees, to a gate behind the giant vampire head, where it couldn't be seen from the sky ride.

"They've lost hope," Pumpkin said. "I guess everyone has."

He spoke quietly into a small black box: "Pumpkin is the best," and the gate creaked open. May watched in amazement, then followed him through. They came to another gate, where he held his face up to a tiny camera perched on the nearest black tree. A laser shot out of it and scanned his eyeball. "Match," a computerized voice said. May's mouth dropped open.

"I had it built last year," Pumpkin said, replying to her expression as they drifted on to a third gate. "You'd be amazed what you have to do to keep out the paparazzi. Thought it'd be a good place to hide from the public eye. And also, go on lots of rides. I never thought I'd be hiding out here for good."

A tiny, sooty creature with pointy ears, a miner's lamp attached to its head, floated out of the keyhole of the gate.

"What is—"

"Tommyknocker," Pumpkin said proudly. "They're very rarely seen or caught. This is one of the few we have in captivity."

"Password?" the tommyknocker squeaked.

Pumpkin looked at May, ready to impress, and then screwed up his face to be very serious and said in a thick British accent, "The rain in Spain falls mainly on the plain."

The tommyknocker bowed, pressing a button that opened the gate. "Welcome home, Your Famousness." As soon as he thought they weren't looking, he set about taking off the hinges of the gate with a tiny screwdriver. Somber Kitty, curled in Pumpkin's arms, let out a low growl.

"I have lots of problems with him," Pumpkin said, "especially with knocking on my walls at night when I'm trying to sleep." He scowled at the tommyknocker's shenanigans, and then his face softened. "But he's just so cute."

May followed him a few steps forward, then paused. Before them was a white house, rambling and crooked. It took May's breath away.

"It's . . ."

"I had them make a replica," Pumpkin said, sighing. "Do you like it?"

"Pumpkin," May breathed, taking it in. A lump of homesickness formed in her throat. "Why?"

The house was an exact duplicate of White Moss Manor: its wide front porch, its dark windows, even its sagging lines. Pumpkin didn't answer May's question; he only led her up the stairs to the porch and through the front door.

"Of course, I had to make a few adjustments," Pumpkin

said, flicking a switch so that a disco ball descended just in front of them, multicolored lights spinning across their faces.

They floated into what would have been the foyer. It was actually a huge room, full of gleaming but yellowed white vinyl furniture and bone white carpet stained all over. Video games lined one wall, with names like Tomb Escape, Zombies on Ice, and Invasion of the Exorcists. There was a foosball table in the corner, a trampoline, and giant art prints of Pumpkin everywhere. The walls, covered in gold lamé, were dominated by awards cases and seventeen huge Silver Spook awards.

He led her into another room, full of bubbles coming from a built-in bubble machine in the ceiling. Here there were four Slurpy Soda machines and chairs made of glassed-in fish tanks with mechanical piranhas swimming about inside. "That's imported mummy gauze." Pumpkin pointed to the tattered curtains. The windows afforded a million-dollar view of Night on Banshee Mountain.

He looked at May eagerly, expectantly. "It's . . . really great." May tried to sound as enthusiastic as possible. It was a little over the top for her.

Pumpkin grinned hugely. He motioned for her to sit down in one of the piranha chairs, and then he sat on her lap, cuddling Kitty close in his arms until the cat finally leaped down. May could feel the piranhas trying to nibble her rear through the upholstery. Somber Kitty swatted at them from the floor.

"So . . . ," May said.

"So . . . ," Pumpkin said, swinging his legs, as if to say, *So what?*

"You were going tell me," May ventured softly, "where are the others?"

"Yep." Pumpkin nodded, still bright, his eyes wide and vacant, as if he was trying to process what he was about to say. And then he flopped over, burying his head in his arms on May's lap.

"First they rnnnghehrererere," he cried. May shifted, alarmed, and tried to keep his elbows from digging into her legs.

"Pumpkin?"

He sat up and sniffled. "And then, and then they . . ." He sniffled again and flopped back down. "Mmnnerereregggu-eruereuregggguguug! Waahhbblebleelbe."

His tears soaked right through May's pajama pants. "Pumpkin." She tapped him on the shoulder. "I can't understand what you're saying."

Pumpkin sat up, gasping. He rubbed his nose holes with the shredded cuff of his sleeve. This was why he had wanted to talk in private, May now realized. He flopped over again. Finally she gave in to just scratching his back and letting him cry, letting him take all the time he needed. Eventually he recovered himself and began to talk in sniffly low tones.

"What happened?" May asked tremulously. She wasn't sure she was ready to hear the answer.

Pumpkin gathered himself slowly and began his story.

"After you left, and we got out of South Place okay, we split up for a while. Beatrice and her mom went to live with the Colony of the Undead, and Fabbio went with them. Lucius went off exploring the realm. I went back to Belle Morte." Pumpkin swallowed.

"When I got back to Beehive House, there was a parchment posted on the door saying I'd been stripped of haunting duties." Pumpkin looked like he was staring right through the floor, sadly. "I couldn't come haunt your house anymore.

"After that I was pretty depressed. I just lolled around without much purpose, doing my chores for Arista. I watched a lot of daytime TV, took up crochet, was really bad at it." He pulled a very poorly crocheted scarf out from underneath his tattered shirt and flashed it at her. "But the weird thing was, sometimes in town, spirits would ask for my autograph. I didn't know why at first, but then I'd go to a restaurant and people would ask me to sing, and eventually it came out that a bunch of spirits had heard of me." Pumpkin brightened. "It was those goblins we sang for, up by the Petrified Pass, spreading the word. Telling everyone about this spectacular talent I have." He shook his head, amazed with himself.

Kitty let out a sigh and looked at May. "Pumpkin," May prodded gently.

Pumpkin blinked back to reality and cleared his throat. "Well, I started doing small gigs in Belle Morte, but the shows were sold out immediately." He sighed theatrically. "You know how that goes. So I got a manager, and he said I should move to Ether, where theater was *really* happening."

"I saw your flyer!" May interjected.

"I've had a good run," Pumpkin replied casually. But then he leaned his chin onto his fist. "Was it my good side? How many did you see?"

"Pumpkin, the others . . ."

Pumpkin sat up. "Right. Well, turns out Lucius was there

now too, with Fabbio and Beatrice, who'd left Isabella with the Colony for safekeeping. Seems they felt useless, hiding out up at the Colony. We got a loft together in Glow-So. Beatrice took in mending. Fabbio frequented the cafés and worked on his poetry. Lucius . . . well . . . liked to put our underwear in the freezer. And then . . ." Pumpkin's spooky face took on a haunted look.

"Pumpkin, what happened?"

Pumpkin stared off into space. "The dark spirits took over. More and more arrived every day. They started taking ghosts away in shackles and replacing all the nice little shops in Ether with chain stores. Horrible, horrible chain stores." He shook his head. "With the worst, cheapest stuff."

He looked dazed for a second, then focused again. "We escaped to Belle Morte, but Arista"—Pumpkin's lips trembled— "was gone. I don't know where. And I left that message for you in the dust, in case you ever came back." He gazed off. "We headed north. But not before . . ."

"What?"

"I saw him once. Bo Cleevil. I mean, really up close. Not like what happened in South Place. He came to watch over the spirits being taken away. You'll never find me next to him again. Never. It's like looking at pure emptiness."

May knew what he meant. She had had more run-ins with Bo Cleevil than any spirit would ever wish. She hoped never to have one again.

"That was about the time Lucius had his idea," Pumpkin finally went on.

"What idea?"

"To sneak into the World of the Living Research Center in Fiery Fork. He had some ideas he'd read about in ghost stories when he was a kid, and sure enough, one of them turned out to be true. They have a transdimensional phone there they've been working on for years." May felt the hairs stand up on the back of her neck. "That was when we started calling you for help."

"Yes!" May nearly shouted. "I got that call! Pumpkin, I heard you! My mom said it was the wires being crossed, but . . ."

Pumpkin nodded, solemnly. And then May had another thought.

"But Pumpkin, that was only weeks ago! Where are the others? They were here?"

"They spotted us on our way out of the research center," he said, barely above a whisper, talking to the floor. "The ghouls. We all ran, but they caught the others. I was the only one who got free." Pumpkin's shoulders sank, like he wanted to shrink too. "They didn't bother as much about me. It's because I'm just a house ghost. They figure I'm harmless."

May's heart broke for Pumpkin. He looked sheepish and small, sitting in his special piranha chair. House ghosts were the lowest of the low in the hierarchy of the Ever After, dimmer than all the rest, their existences full of house chores.

"But I followed them. It didn't really do any good. But I saw the ghouls load them onto a ship docked on the Dead Sea and set sail. Going northeast, I'm sure, like all the other captured souls. They're probably thousands of miles away by now." May reached for his hand, which had flopped down limply at his side. "I couldn't do anything to save them. I guess I *am* harmless."

"That's okay, Pumpkin. You shouldn't have been alone like that." She squeezed his fingers.

"I'm so glad you're here," Pumpkin said, squeezing back, and then he looked like he wanted to say something more. "But I'm really sorry you . . . you know . . ." He made the gesture of a knife across the throat that meant "died."

May went quiet, plucking at her fingernails.

"What's your mom gonna do?" he asked.

May shook her head, her eyes filling with tears. Pumpkin put his hand on her shoulder.

"Like sands through the hourglass," he said solemnly, his own eyes watering, "so are the days of our lives."

"Oh, Pumpkin," said May, smiling in spite of herself.

"Hey," he said, brightening just slightly, putting on a brave face, "you want to see something cool?"

"It was a gift from Queen Elizabeth," Pumpkin said as they floated through a long hall hung with all sorts of keys, Somber Kitty trailing behind them. "Big fan. She loves musicals."

"What are all these for?" May asked.

"Oh." Pumpkin waggled a hand in the air. "Lots of mayors gave me keys to their cities. I've got 'em all, Skull Cross, Bogey Bend . . ."

They drifted past a home movie theater and several parlors, all decorated in different themes: an Arabian Nights room, a Titanic room, a Country & Western room. There was a private telep-a-booth (for sending telepathic messages across the realm) and a room full of gifts Pumpkin had been given by adoring fans: lots of stuffed mummies, dead flowers, two fluorescent pink hearses, a bright orange raft painted with Pumpkin's face (apparently everyone knew he loved to swim), hundreds of packs of Ghouly Gum . . .

"What about the Shakespeare Song & Dance Revue?" May asked. Becoming a member of the Shakespeare Song & Dance Revue was Pumpkin's greatest dream—one he had held for over a hundred years. But Pumpkin stopped dead in his tracks and turned toward her sadly.

"I . . . I auditioned last year, when they came traveling through Ether." He nibbled on the edges of his long white fingers thoughtfully. "Everybody said I was a shoe-in. They said they'd call me if I made it, but . . ."

"Oh, Pumpkin," May said, lowering her voice respectfully. "They didn't call? That's impossible!"

Pumpkin barely had the strength to shake his head. "I guess I just wasn't Shakespeare caliber."

May wrapped her arms around him and squeezed him tight. "They don't know what they're missing," she told him.

"Maybe if I had the chance to audition one more time . . ." Pumpkin's voice trailed off. They both knew there'd be no more auditions for the Shakespeare Song & Dance Revue anytime soon.

May couldn't help thinking of her own dreams. They all required being alive. But she and Pumpkin had each other now. That was something.

"I have to keep it in the pool out back," Pumpkin said, changing the subject and floating forward again.

"What?"

"The gift."

"Pumpkin, what is *it*?"

Pumpkin reached the end of the hall and opened a creaky door onto a wilted lawn. May gasped. Swirling, ducking, and diving in the pool was a beautiful glowing woman, with long brown hair and an orange bikini.

"Is that . . . a water demon?"

Pumpkin laughed. "Nooo. Psssh! Of course not." He rolled his eyes. "Like I would have a water demon in my pool! She's a lorelei." He shrugged. "They lure sailors to their deaths. Distantly *related* to water demons. Great swimmers, of course. Immune to Dead Sea water, even."

"Whoa," May said, staring at the lorelei. She looked too nice to lure sailors to their deaths. She gave May a dazzling white smile.

"Her name's Mona Lisa. You wanna pet her?"

Reluctantly May followed him down to poolside. The lorelei blew water into the air in a thin arc and floated to the side of the pool, staring at Pumpkin expectantly with big glossy eyes.

"She has pretty eyes, don't you think?" As the lorelei fluttered her eyelashes at him, Pumpkin blushed. May couldn't believe it. Pumpkin had fallen in love with a creature that wanted to lure him to his death.

Well, actually, she could believe it. It was almost typical, in fact.

She stared at the lorelei for a long moment, thinking. And then the words shot out of her mouth as fast as they popped into her head.

"Pumpkin, how fast can she swim?"

Chapter Fourteen

Chasing the *Hesperus*

They were packed within minutes. If the ship carrying Lucius, Beatrice, and Fabbio was still crossing the Dead Sea, they didn't have a moment to lose.

May filled a knapsack with supplies she'd found around Pumpkin's mansion: a starlight, a blanket, a compass, a hairbrush (which Pumpkin had insisted on). But when Pumpkin saw the blanket, he shifted from foot to foot, looking uncomfortable.

"You know, spirits don't get cold."

May looked at the blanket, taken by surprise. "Right." She pulled it out of the sack and then laced it over Pumpkin's shoulders. "We'll need a place to go after we take over the ship. Somewhere we can dock."

"We're gonna take over the *ship*?" Pumpkin turned paler than the ghostly pale he already was. "Oh dear."

"I don't think there's any other way."

Pumpkin considered. "Well, there's Portotown. It's the seat of the old ghost stories. Word is that Cleevil hasn't touched it yet, too prestigious—spirits love their celebrities too much. Lots of famous souls. It's, like, the Hollywood of the dead. But it's dangerous. It's close to . . ." Pumpkin's voice trailed off. May knew he meant it was too close to the Platte of Despair, and what lay beyond.

She nodded, pulling back her long hair and tying it in a tight knot at the back of her head. "We'll have to think about it. Meet you back here in five minutes."

She hurried down the hall to the telep-a-booth and stepped inside, closing the door behind her. An envelope appeared in the air over her head. She closed her eyes and tried to concentrate completely, mentally addressing the envelope to the Lady of North Farm. A moment later a piece of paper appeared over her head, awaiting her message.

In desperate need of your help. Stop. Please find us. Stop. May Bird. May looked up in the air. Written on the floating piece of paper were all the words she'd just thought to herself. She crossed her fingers and opened the door of the booth. The message vanished into thin air. She hoped it would find its way.

Pumpkin was sitting with the lorelei, making kissy faces at her. "Hey, cuuuutie," he murmured. "You are sooo cute." He looked up at May. "I hope she's not luring us to our deaths by agreeing to do this."

Kitty sat in a colorful old van parked beside the pool, ads for the Pit of Despair plastered across its surface. He was ready to go, a giant wooden tub loaded in behind him. Pumpkin had strapped a pair of aviator goggles over his eyes—more likely because it looked stylish than to actually help Kitty at all. Still, Kitty licked his chops gamely, looking like a fearless pilot from the 1940s.

Now they just had to get to the Dead Sea. And hope May's idea worked.

"THRILLS! CHILLS! SPILLS! KILLS! COME TO THE PIT OF DESPAIR!"

Slowly they wobbled across the desert.

"Is there any way to turn that down?" May yelled to Pumpkin.

"What?!" he called, cupping his hand to his ear.

May peered into the sky nervously. The Pit of Despair-mobile was topped with a loudspeaker that wouldn't shut off. As if it wasn't conspicuous enough that they were driving a van covered in animatronic mummies that had a spinning skull with flashing purple eyes for a hood ornament. May was sure vampires would appear in the sky at any moment.

She looked over her shoulder at the lorelei, who sat in her tub, grinning at her ambiguously. May could tell why Pumpkin had named her Mona Lisa.

Only the city of Ether punctuated the horizon to the south—small and far away already, its spires soaring as if it were still the city it had been, though a low, dark sky hung above it and gave it a dim, grungy hue.

May felt a huge wave of relief as they reached the immense shore of the Dead Sea, stretching as far as the eye could see to the north and south. But as they climbed out of the van, fear of its dark waters replaced her fear of the vampires. The treacherous water was endlessly vacant before them, not a ship on the horizon and no sign of an opposite shore.

With a splash, the lorelei entered the water.

• • •

The giant orange raft emblazoned with Pumpkin's face sliced through the sea like a knife, the lorelei churning furiously up ahead of them, the sea's hazardous water flying up in their wake. About an hour before, they had lost all sight of land, and now the horizon on every side of them was rippling, oily, and black.

May was beginning to suspect that in this vast ocean, the chances of finding their friends were slim to none. And then a tiny speck appeared in the distance ahead of them. May thought she was imagining it at first. But when she looked over at Pumpkin, he was looking at it too, biting his fingernails.

"Do you think that's it?" he asked.

May pulled one of her arrows from her back and held it ready to string to her bow. "Maybe. Put Kitty in your sack and tie it on tight."

As the speck grew larger, they could see that it was indeed a ship. Whether it was the one they were looking for was a different question. It was a great black galleon, tatty white sails hoisted and blowing in the wind.

The lorelei shot a look back at them and then picked up speed. They coasted forward, faster and faster. May strung her bow and took aim. The wind screamed in her ears, and she trained her eyes on the decks. They could see ghoulish figures now, moving about the boat. And May could see the ship's name, painted on the back: THE HESPERUS. She gasped. Under the dimness of the sky, against the blackness of the sea, the tiniest glow stood out on the prow, like a lamp burning. A glowing figure.

Lucius!

A ghoul standing on the starboard side thrust out an arm toward them, pointing. Two more appeared at the edge and gazed at them, jumping up and down. May pulled her bow back another inch to fire, just as one of the ghouls grabbed Lucius by the scruff of the neck. At that exact moment, May's first arrow flew.

The shot was true. It landed square on the ghoul's chest, and he turned immediately to stone. He tumbled over backward, Lucius disappearing with him.

After that, there was no time to think. In another moment they were upon the ship. They had just enough time to reach out and grab for the ropes hanging off the lower deck before the raft crashed into the boat's massive flank. They scrambled upward, pulling with all their might. And then they were onboard, falling over the rails onto the main deck. Two ghouls saw them and clamored forward. Pumpkin let out a scream. Somber Kitty leaped out of his sack and danced tauntingly, moving like a rubber band. May pointed her arrow at the closest ghoul, which, with a swift shot, she froze to stone immediately. The second got just close enough to reach for her when Kitty jumped on his head, sending him circling and growling and giving May just enough time to string another arrow and shoot. Turning to stone, the ghoul went tumbling off the side of the boat just as Kitty leaped gracefully onto the railing.

A young girl, all in white, emerged from the stairs just behind him, looking baffled, and then her hands flew to her mouth.

"Beatrice, look out!" May dispatched a ghoul behind her.

A tall man with a mustache appeared behind Beatrice. "Mama mia!" he yelled. As they watched in amazement, May turned three more ghouls into stone. Even she was amazed— the arrows went true each time.

Pumpkin was running back and forth on the deck screaming and slapping out blindly with his big, floppy hands. Two ghouls were closing in around him. Threading two arrows into her bow quick as a whip, and tilting them with her fingers in opposite directions, May took them both out at the same time.

Without a word, Bea and Fabbio ran across the decks looking for something to use as weapons, and May sped toward where she had seen Lucius. She found the stone ghoul she had hit first, knocked over sideways, and one pale, luminous arm waving at her from the floor underneath him.

"Lucius!"

The arm waggled and waved. May could see now that the stone ghoul still had him tightly by the scruff of the neck. "Mm mmmant mooove!" Lucius yelled.

May pushed hard against the statue, but it didn't budge.

"Gblblblblb!"

May turned, placing one foot protectively on the stone ghoul as three ghouls advanced toward her.

She drew her bow and hit the first just as he stepped forward. The other two came to a halt, looked at her, then looked at each other and jumped over the side of the ship, howling as they went. May stood where she was, poised for the next attack, waiting.

For a moment things were quiet. Bea and Fabbio appeared by her side, holding long planks of wood in their arms like bats, looking around, unsure.

May shot fierce, searching looks in all directions, brushing back her dark hair, which had wildly tumbled out of its knot. Somber Kitty appeared in the crow's nest above them and meowed, as if to say, *All clear.*

"Pumpkin?" May called nervously.

"Present!" Pumpkin emerged from inside a barrel that stood right beside her.

"Is there anyone else back there?" she asked Fabbio. He disappeared down the stairs, then reappeared a moment later, shaking his head.

Beatrice stood gaping at May. She looked the same as the day May had left—long white dress, blue sash, pale and spectral and Victorian. She drifted toward her unsurely. "Is it . . . really you? You've . . . you're so tall. . . ."

May nodded. "It's me."

Bea's tapered white hands flew to her mouth, and tears of joy welled up in her eyes. In another moment she had wrapped her arms around May and was holding her tight. Suddenly they were both tackled from the side and wrapped up in Fabbio's arms. He hugged them like a daddy longlegs.

"It'sa May a come to save us! I knewa you would come!" He reached out his gangly arms and pulled Pumpkin into the hug too.

May felt relief wash through her. Here she was, finally. *Among friends.* Among the people who believed her journey to the Ever After was real. Believed *in* her. Understood her best. All her years back in Briery Swamp, May had forgotten how this felt.

"But May," Beatrice pulled back, "you're so cold."

"Urggghhh."

They all looked down at Lucius. He was stuck on his side,

looking in the direction of the sea, his cheek flush against the floor. May knelt beside him and for a moment studied the stone hand that gripped him. "I don't know how to get you out of this," she said.

"Karate chop the stone," Pumpkin suggested.

"Mew," Kitty agreed, appearing beside her, only to be immediately scooped up in Fabbio's passionate embrace.

"That might break his neck," said Beatrice.

"Broken neck is no big deal," Fabbio offered helpfully. "He wear a nice tie, look handsome." Lucius let out a groan. His face had gone bright red; he was clearly frustrated.

"Gggurrrgle!"

May bit her lip, thinking. She crossed the deck, swooped up a bucket, and then found a rope. While everyone looked on, bewildered, she lowered the bucket into the Dead Sea, ever so carefully, and raised it again once it was full. Biting her tongue, she lowered it onto the deck as if it were a bomb. "Watch out," she whispered, grabbing a rag from the deck and dipping it gingerly into the water, so that her fingers remained far from the side that was wet.

She then carried the dripping cloth toward Lucius, the others clearing to either side to let her pass.

"Urrrgggh," Lucius protested.

May carefully dangled the cloth over the ghoul's stone arm, so that one tiny droplet of water tumbled onto its surface. She whipped the cloth away with a magician-like flourish, at the same moment the stone ghoul disappeared entirely—no doubt reappearing immediately in South Place, miles below them. Lucius lay curled in a ball now, utterly free.

He rolled onto his back, rubbing his neck. Then he looked up at her, his blue eyes wide. Lucius, like everyone else, was the same age he'd been when she'd left—thirteen. His usually pinkish cheeks were red from exertion, but he was still as filled with soft white light as ever. He wore his old-fashioned school uniform—gray jacket and pants and a maroon tie. "You're . . ."

"Dead," May said softly, laying the cloth on top of a nearby barrel.

Beatrice gasped, her hands flying to her heart. Fabbio cleared his throat, uncomfortable.

Lucius was the only one not distressed by the news. He shook his head, standing up and rubbing the arm he'd been lying on. "I was going to say older." He cleared his throat, as if he was embarrassed.

"Yeah." May swallowed. She reached out a hand and he looked at it, then grasped it to shake. She didn't know why she didn't hug him. "Nice to see you again, Lucius," she said.

"Likewise." Lucius bowed, as if remembering some long-lost manners that didn't fit him anymore. "Of course"—he cleared his throat and let her hand drop—"I was planning our escape from this ship." He grabbed a spear from the deck and cut a dashing figure.

"It didn't look like it," Bea said. Lucius scowled at her, his glow turning a brownish angry color.

"Nonsense," he said matter-of-factly, holding up the spear so he could expertly examine the sharpness of its tip with his fingers. "Girls are just too foolish to know when they're about to be saved."

"And I suppose it makes no difference that a *girl* just saved you," Beatrice retorted, drifting to May's side and looping her arm through hers companionably.

Lucius looked at May, squinted, and blushed, then went back to examining his spear.

"May, what happened? How did you die?" Beatrice asked, overjoyed and overwrought at the same time.

"Um, guys . . . ," Pumpkin said.

"She's even prettier than before, isn't she, Captain?" added Bea.

Lucius rolled his eyes and did a few more fearsome poses with the spear. Captain Fabbio nodded enthusiastically, twirling his mustache.

"Guys." Pumpkin tapped May on the shoulder.

"Beauty like the moon over Sicily in September!" Fabbio exclaimed. "I gotta poem that goes—"

"ROCK!" They both turned to look at Pumpkin, who'd screamed at the top of his lungs.

Sure enough, they were being pulled straight toward a giant, craggy rock slicing out of the water's surface. A beautiful nude woman lay sunbathing on the rock's surface, waving at them. May had a moment to glance over the side of the boat, where the lorelei backstroked, grinning at her, her rope tied to the bow of the ship.

Lucius lunged for the wheel. May grabbed her arrows and shot one right through the rope that the lorelei was using to pull them. Then she fell on the wheel next to Lucius.

As they worked furiously to turn the ship, May could hear Pumpkin up ahead, calling to the beautiful woman on the rocks. "Hey, there! Do you know who I am? Did you see *Drifty*

Dancing Two? The guy in the band at the cabana scene?"

Fabbio perched at the very prow of the boat, standing tall and pointing left, like a sea captain or a hunting dog, as if pointing was very important. "Left!" he kept shouting.

The ship came about slowly. They watched breathlessly as its prow glided just left of the rocks and then passed smoothly out of harm's way.

There was a collective exhalation of relief along the deck.

Everyone but Lucius, who was still steering, leaned to peer over the side at the disaster they had just averted. The rock, and its beautiful sunbather, got smaller and smaller behind them.

"Wow, how would you like to be shipwrecked on a rock?" May said, gazing at its numerous spiky, deadly outcroppings, and the vast and empty sea that surrounded it.

"That wasn't a rock," Bea replied softly. "That was the Isle of the Water Demons."

Pumpkin traipsed back along the deck as the isle drifted away, dazzled. "They looked friendly enough," he said wistfully.

The bikini-clad lorelei lit up and, as if in reply, hundreds of lights came on just under the surface of the water around her. May's stomach turned sickly as she realized that they were all demons too, and she thought of the fate they had just avoided. Her heart skipped a beat.

Well, it would have, if it had still been beating.

Chapter Fifteen

Choices

"I hear it's full of spies," Beatrice said.

They were sitting in a circle at the front of the boat. It was completely dark. Bea had explained that they were nearing the Ever After's northern pole, which was the only place in the entire realm where one got a view of the single moon that floated above. They had caught each other up, in bursts of laughter and moments of tears, on the things that had happened while they'd been apart. When Beatrice talked of her mother, she spent the time carefully arranging the folds of her tattered white dress, trying to keep her composure. "I'm sure she's all right," she kept saying. "I'm sure the Colony must be all right."

When May recounted how she died, the others looked on sympathetically, knowing—with the exception of Pumpkin, who had never been alive at all—what it was like to lose a gift as precious as life. Beatrice reached for her hand several times and insisted she didn't need to say any more. But it felt good to get it out.

They discussed Bo Cleevil in whispers, as if he might be drifting in the shadows above, watching them. Everyone had heard in some shape or form about his plans for the Cleevilvilles and invading the Earth. May thought of everything she knew on Earth, everything precious and safe, her mom, her beloved woods full of shadows and birds and insects. She had tried to picture those same woods filled with ghouls, and zombies, and goblins—ghouls invading the house where her mom slept—and the image struck dread into her, right down to the tips of her toes.

Now Fabbio stood at the wheel, looking at the moon and singing softly to himself in Italian. May wondered what he was singing about—he looked so forlorn. But then, in a way, they all did. Forlorn . . . and relieved to finally have one another.

By the map that Beatrice had dug from the galley, they knew they were in the remotest part of the Dead Sea. Portotown was at the northeastern edge, many leagues ahead of them. Beyond it the Platte of Despair was clearly marked, but beyond that, the map ended.

"So the decision really is," May said, "what do we do now? Do we want to go somewhere and hide, or . . ."

Everyone knew what she was thinking. It was clear by the solemn looks on their faces, but she had to say it.

"Or do we continue to head north, to Portotown . . . toward Bo Cleevil . . . and try to do something."

"There are only five of us," Bea said.

"Mew," protested Kitty.

"I mean six," she corrected herself.

"But there's the Lady," May said. "She'll find us. And then we'll have a chance." She tugged thoughtfully at the fabric of her bathing suit. "I don't know. I don't know what the right thing to do is. I just know I don't want to go back to hiding. I don't want to go back to doing *nothing*."

"I'm not scared," Lucius declared, puffing out his chest a little.

"I hear the slimer ghosts from that movie *Ghostbusters* live in Portotown," Pumpkin offered. "I wouldn't mind getting their autographs. They've probably heard of me."

"Those ghosts weren't real, Pumpkin," May offered.

But Pumpkin gave her a patronizing look. "I saw them with my own two eyes. On *TV*. Hel*lo*."

May and Bea grinned at each other. Bea had never seen a TV, because she had died of typhoid in 1911, long before they'd been invented. But they had spent many nights sleeping side by side next to campfires and walking endless hours in the desert, and May had told her lots of things about the modern world.

"I think Casper lives there too," Pumpkin muttered thoughtfully.

"We have a few more hours to decide," Bea finally said, "before we need to tack left or right. Maybe we should think about it till then."

They all agreed. As they talked about other things, catching up on the last few years, their hearts all weighed heavy with their decision. And though nobody mentioned it, none of them saw any hope until the Lady had found them.

That night May, Pumpkin, and Somber Kitty sat on the ship's deck, keeping watch. Fabbio, Bea, and Lucius had gone to sleep down below. The sky was dark as midnight, but a glow penetrated the dark from somewhere unseen. A cold northern breeze blew across the boat.

"Have you heard of the Bridge of Souls?" May asked, petting Kitty, who slept on her lap.

Pumpkin nodded.

"Will you tell me about it?"

Pumpkin was quiet for a while. "A lot of spirits say it doesn't exist. Other spirits, the crunchy granola ones, say that you can't find it, *it has to find you.*" He rolled his eyes. "They also eat a lot of tofu. Talk about feng shui and all that."

"What is it?"

Pumpkin stuck his long white fingers into his mouth thoughtfully, then pulled them out. "It's the bridge to whatever's after . . . the Ever After. Once you cross it you can never ever come back."

May swallowed. Finally she said, "Do *you* think it exists?"

Pumpkin shrugged. "I wouldn't want to find out. Nobody knows where it leads. Spirits say you become something else when you cross."

"Maybe you become something . . . *amazing.*"

"Maybe not."

"Maybe things aren't so scary on the other side," May said hopefully.

Pumpkin smoothed his yellow tuft of hair. "Pssh. *The other side.* Sounds pretty scary to me."

They sat quietly for a few minutes. May thought of her mom, imagining May on the *other side.*

"Sometimes I think . . . ," Pumpkin said, then stopped.

"What?"

"It's stupid."

May leaned forward and took his hand. "You can tell me."

"Sometimes I get this bad feeling. Like this is our last trip together."

May squeezed his fingers. "I'm sure you're just nervous."

Pumpkin smoothed out his tuft with his free hand. "Maybe."

An hour or so later, Lucius appeared behind them, glowing warmly like a firefly. He was followed by Beatrice and Fabbio.

"Well, we thought it's probably time," Lucius said. "If we're heading to Portotown, we'll need to tack soon. And, well . . ."

May and Pumpkin stood up. They all hovered in a sort of messy circle, silently shifting on their feet.

Lucius stuck his hands in his trouser pockets. But for his ghostly translucence, he looked the very picture of a boy who should be off playing a game of cricket, or studying for an exam. "What have we got to lose but the rest of our afterlives?" he said.

By the way everyone nodded and murmured, May knew they were all in agreement.

"We should call ourselves something," Pumpkin suggested, but for the moment, no one could think of what.

Lucius smiled slightly at May. She smiled back. They turned and faced across the watery path ahead of them. Fabbio drifted to the captain's wheel. The moon, an amazing sight in the Ever After, had just risen over the horizon, casting a swath of white light across the black water, as if it were guiding them.

They all watched it, enchanted, as they steered a course for Portotown.

Chapter Sixteen

Portotown

ing, ding, ding.

The passengers of the *Hesperus* jumped to hear the hollow, haunting sound of a buoy being tossed about on the sea. They leaped from where they'd been lying, or sitting, for the past few hours and looked over the front of the boat.

A deep fog surrounded them, so that they could only just make out the buoy that floated a few feet away, bobbing back and forth. A few pinprick lights glimmered in the distance. May lifted Kitty and tucked him into her sack.

Over the next several minutes, as they all looked on eagerly, the port began to take shape—a wide wooden dock, several ships roped to its pilings, spirits bustling all over its surface: burly ship hands practically bursting out of their long-sleeved shirts, sacks slung over their shoulders or else carrying barrels between them or unloading trunks down the gangways.

May watched, wide-eyed, as they drifted into port and a group of men grabbed the ropes dangling off the sides of their ship and tied them to the nearest pilings. Pumpkin stuck his hand in hers and bit the nails of his other hand. When the boat was fully secured, they all drifted down the gangway and made their way through the bustling spirits on the dock.

As soon as they reached the cobbled square at the end, a man went galloping past within a hairsbreadth of them on what appeared to be an invisible horse, nearly running them over. They jumped out of the way and then turned to watch him. He was riddled with bullet holes, and a bunch of lace flopped at his throat as he rode off into the darkness. "A highwayman," Beatrice whispered, awed. "They're very dangerous."

Above them the moon resembled a ghostly galleon tossed upon cloudy seas. Carriages drawn by invisible horses bustled in all directions down the foggy, cobblestoned streets. The horsemen were all headless, steering carriages down alleys. The streets were lined with old stone mansions, surrounded by spiky wrought-iron fences, their bottom floors illuminated and the attic-level windows dark, the curtains of these floors moving as if someone in each house was looking out at them. Lightning flashed above. Ladies in tattered dresses and straw hats promenaded along the docks, carrying baskets full of dead roses for sale. One drifted past them and gave them a meaningful look. "Wicked night," she said.

They all looked at one another, spooked. "I bet they always say that," Pumpkin said fliply, wagging a hand. May felt Somber Kitty tremble at her back.

They wove their way down the road, gazing at every apparition, awed by the sheer number of creepy specters.

Suddenly Lucius grabbed the backs of their clothes and dragged them into an alley, hissing "Vampire!" Their hearts in their throats, they pressed themselves against the brick wall of the alley, watching the street breathlessly. A moment later a pale, polished man in a black cape drifted past. He moved with oily composure, like a true gentleman, his hands pale and unblemished at his sides, his posture perfect. His face was stony, pale, and merciless. He floated onward slowly, deliberately.

"He's patrolling," Bea whispered, sending chills down May's arms. "All vampires in the realm are on the lookout for trouble-makers. They bring them directly to Bo Cleevil's fortress."

The group waited several seconds after he had passed before they dared to peek around the corner after him. They just saw the tail of his cape as he vanished down the street into the fog. They entered the street again, this time a little more cautiously, and continued onward, floating past a car guarded by old-fashioned soldiers carrying bayonets, all with mustaches. The car bumped and bucked, its lights flashing on and off.

Fabbio pulled his mustache and nodded at them like a general.

"Possessed cars," Bea whispered to May, who watched the car in wonder. "They're the worst on gas mileage."

"Hey, that looks like a good spot." Lucius pointed.

They all looked at a modest, crooked wooden house up ahead, a sign hanging out front that announced THE SLEEPING SPECTER INN. May agreed—it would be a relief to get off the spooky street and make their plans. They drifted toward it.

Inside, a warm fire blazed in a rustic tavern room full of wooden tables, a red rug, and a bearskin stretched and hanging above the hearth. A woman sat at one table, leaning her chin thoughtfully on a gleaming arm, reading a book. The inn-keeper was wiping down another table. He looked up at them. "Wicked night out," he said in a deep English accent. "Welcome." And then he went back to cleaning.

"Ooh, that woman has a golden arm," Pumpkin whispered to May. "Lucky."

May elbowed him. "Don't stare." The sound of loud, rickety carriage wheels carried in from the street.

"I saya we stay here. Like my uncle Bonino always say—," Fabbio started.

"Ooh," Bea interrupted, tugging May's arm and pulling her to the window. "It's Lady Howard!"

May peered out beside her. A fearsome carriage had just parked in front of the tavern across the street. It looked to be made of human bones. From its dark window stared a gaunt specter, filmy and gray, her bluish lips pursed together in a frown, her eyes wide and vacant.

"Who's Lady Howard?" May breathed, awed.

"A murderess." Bea's blue eyes opened wide for emphasis. "She rides around in a carriage made of the bones of her four dead husbands. She has to ride around picking blades of grass until every blade is gone." Bea took a deep breath. "Basically, until the world ends."

Beatrice, scaring herself, wrapped her arm around May's but couldn't tear her eyes from the carriage.

"Can I show you to your rooms?" the innkeeper asked, making them jump. When they realized it was only him, they looked at each other and broke into relieved giggles.

May and Bea's room was done in red velvet with a red hurricane lamp and long red velvet curtains. May pulled them aside to look out her window. In the back, bathed in the moonlight, was a graveyard. She gazed out at it, then up at the moon.

While Kitty curled peacefully upstairs, the group headed down to the parlor and stayed late into the night, playing cards and enjoying the fire. They turned in around midnight, bleary-eyed. But May and Bea couldn't help sitting up even later, talking. Somber Kitty kept popping one eye open at them to let them know he was trying to sleep. They shot him apologetic looks and tried to keep their voices low.

"Have you heard anything from the spirits of Risk Falls?" May asked. Risk Falls was a sublime oasis they had stumbled onto while journeying across the Hideous Highlands. Its spirits were reckless and bold, but when it had come to defending the realm against Bo Cleevil, it became clear that they weren't as brave as they seemed.

Bea shook her head sadly. "No. I telep-a-grammed them a few times, but nothing. I—"

Knock, knock. All three of them, Somber Kitty included, stared at the door. May looked at Bea, who shook her head to indicate that she had no idea who it could be.

May stood up and floated over to peer through the keyhole. All she could see was the waist of a black suit. She looked at Beatrice. "Maybe it's a message from the Lady!" she whispered. And then, holding her breath, she opened the door a crack. It creaked ominously. "Yes?" she warbled.

A butler with a gaunt face and long, skinny sideburns stood in the hallway. "A note for you, madame," he said, handing her a yellowed piece of paper. May snatched it out of his hand excitedly.

She unfolded it and read a short note scrawled in bloodred ink, her shoulders sinking.

May Bird and date. The pleasure of your company is requested by Her Highness the Duchess of Lauderdale at the palace ball, tomorrow evening, nine p.m.

She looked up at the butler, bewildered.

He nodded his head respectfully, pursing his blue lips. "I suggest you go, madame. It's in your best interest."

May blinked at him a few times. "My best interest?"

The butler didn't answer. He simply bowed and moved down the hall, perfectly erect.

May watched him go, and then drifted inside and showed the note to Beatrice.

"You should go," Bea said solemnly.

May stared down at the letter. "Why would I go? We're supposed to be here secretly."

"May, the Duchess of Lauderdale is quite famous. In life, she murdered her husband. And I hear she can be equally unkind to people who decline her invitations." Bea paused, then made a slicing motion across her throat.

"Oh," May said, rubbing her neck and swallowing. "Oh?"

"It's just the way things are done. And I think, well, specters in Portotown are too self-absorbed to know who you are. I doubt they read the papers, and you've grown so . . ." Bea took the letter and stared at it a moment longer, tapping the word "date" with her petite index finger. "The question is not if you are going to go, but who are you going to bring?"

"I'd really rather not." Pumpkin was lounging on his bed the next morning, his hands behind his head. May stood with her letter at her side, her big brown eyes pleading. "Everybody'll recognize me. They'll make me do the whole song and dance, and then another song and dance. They only ever want to hear the big hits." He sighed. "You go ahead without me. I'm *used* to big fancy parties. *You'll* enjoy it."

"Meow?"

May looked down at Kitty. "I don't think they allow banished species as dates," she muttered sadly.

"You should bring Lucius," Pumpkin went on, gesturing carelessly toward Lucius, who sat in the windowsill making a slingshot to sling ectoplasm balls at passing specters. This seemed to annoy Fabbio no end, and he kept glancing up at Lucius, his mustache twitching.

May and Lucius looked at each other. Lucius dimmed, then scowled. May looked away, tightening her ponytail and running her fingers through her long black hair.

After a minute or so, Lucius sighed. He plucked at his slingshot restlessly. "Do I have to get dressed up?"

"Probably," Pumpkin threw in, before May could answer.

"Can I bring my slingshot?"

"No," May said firmly.

He considered, his blue eyes thoughtful. "Okay. I'll do it."

May felt a leap of excitement. "Okay."

Heading back to her room, May felt mixed up inside. For all her confusion, and fear, and uncertainty, she couldn't help smiling. She was about to go on her very first date.

Chapter Seventeen

The Duchess's Ball

As the carriage pulled into the semicircular drive that scooped in front of the palace, May knew there were important things that were supposed to be on her mind, like the Lady of North Farm, and Bo Cleevil's plans to invade the world of the living. But as she caught sight of the big, dazzling bonfires that lit the way to the palace, and the carriages ahead of them, she felt dizzy with excitement. May had never been to a ball.

The huge palace—three graceful stories of white marble—was stately, noble, and very old, with large marble pillars holding it up. Its vast front verandah and stairs were lit by torches so that it beckoned festively to passersby, the fires sending cheerful shadows dancing across the stone. In the windows above, the curtains occasionally moved as shadowy figures marked the arrivals below.

"It looks like everyone compared notes before they came," May said worriedly. She watched the other guests disembarking in the queue ahead of them: The ladies all in bright, if moldy, colors—pink and blue and spring green silks, with bunches of ripped lace hanging out of the cuffs and bodices.

The most magnificent costumes were the moldiest and most decrepit, and these spectresses held their heads high, their chins pointed into the air. The gentlemen wore pastel suits with lace handkerchiefs. Everyone wore powdered white wigs, laced with cobwebs and decorated with bits of dead flowers.

May looked down at her own dress. Pumpkin had helped her pick it out that afternoon. It was thick black velvet, soft as cat's fur, with sparkling star-shaped buttons along the bodice, crisscrossed with silken threads as silvery as moonlight. It was covered in dusty cobwebs, sending puffs of dust flying off the fabric every time she moved. The velvet made her hair—combed straight and glossy down her back—look so black it become lost beneath her shoulders, like night. Her neck was strung with ancient pearls, tiny pendants encrusted with rubies, and dripping emeralds.

Lucius had not eased her self-consciousness in the least. The whole ride, he'd given her legs and arms twisty pinches and stuck his wet pinky in her ear when she wasn't looking. Now he was swinging his legs and looking out the window restlessly, as if he'd rather be anywhere else. Glowing on the seat next to her in his school uniform, he looked even more out of place than May did. He had at least, she noticed, brushed his hair. And he looked very handsome, though May would never have told him that.

"I should have worn something else," May whispered, mortified, scrunching up her birdlike white shoulders and feeling, among other things, entirely too tall. Lucius seemed to wake from his daze and looked over at her a tad softly, then at the lovely and decrepit ladies gliding up the stairs.

He wrinkled his nose. "You look *worlds* better than those old bags," he said.

"Gee, thanks."

In another few moments their carriage was next in line and lurched up to the walkway. May and Lucius climbed down from the carriage, May's stomach full of butterflies, and they floated up the path. May looked at all the other couples, their arms linked together. But she couldn't bring herself to link her arm through Lucius's. They reached the stairs. The elegant, gilded doors of the mansion creaked open, and two skeletal doormen in livery grinned at them eyelessly as they drifted inside. The doors closed behind them.

Gazing around, May felt like she had floated into a dream. They were in an enormous ballroom—as sumptuous as velvet. Candelabras hung from the ceiling of the dusty, tapestry-covered hallway, illuminating everything in warm light. An orchestra at the far end of the room played lopsided, off-key classical music. Beautiful specters in elaborate dress, draped in decorative cobwebs, swayed back and forth just above the floor. And above it all, on a marble platform, in a chair made of gold and tattered silk brocade, sat a woman May could only presume was the duchess herself. Her hair was pulled into a great pouf that towered a foot above her head and was adorned with ruby spiders. She held a silver-tipped cane in one hand and swept the room with murderous eyeballs, one of which was covered with a monocle.

May looked at Lucius to share her amazement, but his eyes were pinned to the tables of sweets by the band: piles of coffin-shaped chocolates filled with Grimy Ganache, and glimmering plates stacked with all sorts of tiny, delectable cakes made to look like miniature, sugary graveyards. There were roasts decorated with blood red sauce, pies shaped like bats, and towering black fountains of gooey black drool with severed-finger crackers for dipping. A specter who looked uncannily like Henry the Eighth appeared to be flirting with a young woman by a dilapidated harpsichord in the corner. An inordinate number of guests carried their heads under one arm, and May was sure she recognized Marie Antoinette from a picture in her fifth-grade history book.

Several specters turned to look at them. May shifted from foot to foot, unsure what to do, hoping against hope that no one recognized her as the ten-year-old girl in the shroud whose picture had been plastered across the newspapers three years ago, and whose image hung on WANTED signs all over the city of Ether. And besides, she had no idea how to behave at parties. She took courage from knowing Lucius was by her side. At least she didn't have to face the crowd alone.

"Ooh, Creaky Cookies," Lucius breathed, and in a moment he had zipped off in a ball of light. May stared after him, her mouth dropping open, adrift.

"Wicked night, isn't it?" someone said behind her. She turned. A man in a silk brocade coat and white wig stood behind her, sipping daintily at a glass of black liquid.

"Yes, yes." Another specter nodded as they moved to include May in their circle. This, apparently, was the way things were done at balls. May nodded politely.

"Yes," she muttered too.

"The wickedest night I ever saw," a gentleman with a

handlebar mustache began regally, "was when I was eaten by the pygmies in Papua New Guinea in 1893. . . ."

The music played on, and as May listened politely to the endless talk of horrible deaths and the weather, she noticed that many eyes were drifting to her repeatedly. A cold shiver ran down her spine. She soon began to hear snippets of comments about her dress, about Lucius (who was now tangled in a curtain behind the piano, it seemed, dropping Itchy Dust in Marie Antoinette's hair), about the Sleeping Specter Inn where she was staying. The mustachioed man went on and on, pointing to a man in the corner he said was Ferdinand Magellan and relating an adventure they'd had with poltergeists in Booey Butte in their early dead days. May began to drift off, gazing at the people around her who were gazing at her, wondering what they knew. . . .

"My dear?"

May realized she was being addressed. She looked at a headless woman standing across from her, then looked down in the direction of her waist. The woman's head, with a high white wig and a big mole near the nose, was staring at her.

"Excuse me?" May asked, flustered.

"Haven't I seen you somewhere?" the head asked politely, with an upper-crusty sniffle.

May lowered her head. She swallowed, feeling her neck and face flush crimson. "I don't think so."

"I'm sure that I have," the head insisted. "In a newspaper, or . . . ?"

May looked about uneasily, feeling behind her instinctively for her bow, which of course she had secreted at the inn. A circle of other spirits, several of them headless, had gravitated around them and were now listening curiously. Clearly they had been waiting for this.

"Yes yes, I remember, it was in the *Spectator.*" The head looked pleased with herself. She looked like she was always pleased with herself. May sucked in her breath and held it, glancing toward the front door. If she grabbed Lucius now . . . "You were at the premiere of *Drifty Dancing Two*, weren't you?"

To May's shock, several of the other spirits murmured agreement.

May let out the breath. "No, I—"

"Yes, yes, useless to deny it. You were there on the arm of . . . who was it, that old scoundrel." The woman smiled wryly. "Julius Caesar."

"No," a specter in a monocle interrupted. The monocle sat over an eye that was completely dangling out. May stiffened. "That's not who you're thinking of at all. She looks an awful lot like that Live One, that girl." He paused, and May could feel her whole body flaming up. "You're much prettier, obviously, but *you* know the one I'm thinking of"—he snapped his fingers in the air thoughtfully—"the one who's supposed to . . . oh, what is she supposed to do?"

"Save the Ever After from certain doom?" May blurted out in frustration, before she could stop herself. The circle of painted faces blinked at her for a few moments. The dangling eye would have blinked if it had had eyelids. May could have kicked herself.

One woman, her head tilting unnaturally to one side from where she'd been hanged, opened her mouth to say something, thought better of it, and then went ahead anyway. "Have you ever tried doing something with your hair?"

The air went out of May like a balloon.

From there, the conversation circled like a restless bee: which royal was dating her executioner, which nonroyals had been seen skinny-dipping in the Bog of Misery, electromagnetic massage and whether it really worked . . .

Now that the danger had seemingly passed, it was dawning on May that her first ball was turning out to be stupendously . . . boring. And even a little depressing. Everyone in Portotown seemed to care more about the business of everyone else in Portotown than they did about the fate of their world.

She looked again for Lucius, who appeared to be enjoying himself immensely. With the usual mischievous twinkle in his eye, he was stuffing handfuls of Spiky Stabbies surreptitiously into spirits' knickerbockers, biting his lip to keep from smiling too widely. She longed to join him. It would beat hearing about how Napolean had had exoskeletal surgery to make his soul taller, and who was prettier, the Maharaja or Helen of Troy.

May needed air. She waited for a lull in the conversation and then politely excused herself, hurrying to the glass doors at the back of the room before someone could accost her and slipping outside with a sigh of relief. Turning around as she closed the door behind her, she sighed again, forgetting the room behind her entirely, enchanted. She was in a lovely moonlit garden, as sweet and refreshing as the indoors had been stifling and stuffy. Across the finely clipped lawn, glistening silver in the moonlight, lay a labyrinth, lined with hedges. Its stony path invited her to disappear inside. May glanced back through the doors, then floated forward.

The path under her feet glowed like it had been sprinkled with fairy dust. The garden was a world away from the Cleevil-villes and all the ruin they had seen stretching across the Ever After. Soon, she knew, there would be no magic left like this. By now, there was probably no New Egypt, or Fiery Fork, or Stabby Eye. And soon there would be no house ghosts like Pumpkin, or colorful specters like Lady Howard, or even wild and woolly spirits like poltergeists. It would be like the colors of the Ever After had slipped off into the atmosphere.

And then Bo Cleevil would move on to Earth and ruin the beautiful things there, too.

May had reached the very center of the labyrinth, and here she stopped short. A man was sitting on a stone bench, pensively studying the moon. He wore a white dusted wig and a long blue jacket. He looked up just as May started to back away.

"Sorry," May mumbled, retreating.

"No no . . . please don't let me deter you from enjoying the garden."

His face was powdered and smooth. He had very nice spectral features, all in the right place—straight lines making up his nose and his jaw, his eyes big and windowlike. He was, in fact, very handsome.

May stopped, hesitated, drifted forward.

"Please . . ." He gestured to the bench. May thought for a moment, then sat.

"You're not enjoying the party?" he asked.

May looked over her shoulder. "No, it's fine. . . ."

The specter sighed, ennui settling over his fine features. "These parties are always a bore. Always spirits gabbing about nothing very important. I've always felt," he said, tucking a hand into his coat, "very far away at parties."

May nodded. She knew the feeling.

"Sometimes I think one is better off staying home," he said.

"Sometimes you can't go home," May murmured, without really meaning to.

The spirit smiled, gently, as if he understood. "The problem with leaving home is that, even when you go back, you're never really completely home again."

May didn't reply. The stranger studied her.

"If you'll permit me to say it, I think that you look quite lost."

May looked up at him, surprised, and then she plucked at her fingers. If she were honest, she'd have to say she'd always felt a little lost.

"Some souls don't belong anywhere," the specter next to her offered casually, as if reading her mind. "Are you one of those?"

May didn't reply. She kicked her feet at the dusty path. "Do you know about the Bridge of Souls?" she finally asked.

The stranger nodded.

She sighed. She looked up at the moon. "Do you think if you cross it, you stop being afraid?"

The stranger turned toward her, intrigued. "What is it you're afraid of?"

May shrugged. She wasn't exactly sure. At home she had been afraid of not being like everyone else, and of never fitting. Now she was afraid of much bigger things. She was scared of what she was supposed to do, and afraid she didn't know the right way to do it.

"You know, if you come with me, you'll never have to be afraid."

May felt the hairs on the back of her neck stand up. It was an instinct.

"When you have everything, you *always* belong."

The stranger gazed at her, and for the first time May let herself meet his eyes. They were clear and blue, but there was something else. They were empty.

"We will find each other," the stranger said. "It's inevitable."

May went to stand up, but he put one cold hand on hers. It passed right through her fingers. "I'm not going anywhere."

May looked over her shoulder, as if someone may come to help her, then back at him. He smiled.

"Who are you looking for? The Lady? I'm afraid she's no longer here."

May knew, with every fiber, that the hand reaching for her was the hand of Bo Cleevil, and that the empty eyes were his eyes.

"You haven't even seen the beginning of how scary I can be," he said.

"Hey," a voice said behind her. "Who are you talking to?"

May turned. Lucius stood there, two plates of spidercake in his hands. May swiveled to look at the bench again. The man was gone.

Goosebumps raced up and down her arms. She still felt like someone was standing nearby, invisible, watching.

Even out of sight, it seemed he was all around her.

Chapter Eighteen

Escape from Portotown

H e'll be on his way now."

They were gathered in the parlor of the Sleeping Specter, huddled up near the window that looked out on to the street. Every few minutes Fabbio pulled the curtains back to peek, then quickly closed them.

It was determined, as soon as May had told them what she had seen, that Bo Cleevil had simply bilocated—he had managed to be in two places at once. Spirits sometimes did this when they were looking for something or trying to communicate a message—one part of themselves would stay wherever they were, and the other part would go off and search, or deliver the message that the other half didn't have time for. Now that Bo Cleevil had found her, he was sure to send the vampires for them, or worse, come himself.

"We should get out of here, move west. Find a place to hide out until we can contact the Lady," Lucius said, his eyes darting from time to time to the windows.

"But he'll find us before we can get anywhere fast enough," Beatrice pointed out.

May considered. They were so close to the Platte of Despair

and Bo Cleevil's castle beyond. And it seemed that to run away now would be to leave the possibility of *doing something* behind. She just didn't know what that something would be. Without the Lady's help, it was impossible to know.

She stood and looked out the windows. No sign of vampires yet. "There's got to be a way to get out fast."

"There's only one way I can think of," Bea said, her eyes alight. "But it's not pleasant."

After Beatrice had explained her idea, May pulled out her arrows. Lucius pulled out his slingshot. Somber Kitty ran to wake Pumpkin from his three o'clock nap. Fabbio pulled out his compass and cleared his throat, waiting for orders. May tugged back the curtain one more time to check that what they needed was still there.

Moments later they were racing across the street and surrounding Lady Howard's bony carriage.

In one quiet, deft move May threw open the left-hand door and drew her bow. Lady Howard, to her surprise, only stared at her from her bench seat, a twisted smile playing about her pinched lips.

"Um, can you please get out?" May whispered to her (so much for being a wild bandit), but Lady Howard didn't so much as blink. May leaned back to check that they were still in the clear, her stomach aching with fear. And then Pumpkin let out a whimper, and May's eyes lit on what she most feared, floating down the alley toward them. The vampire was staring out at the sea, his long fangs gleaming under his pale lips. He hadn't noticed them yet.

"I think it's impossible for her to leave the carriage," Bea whispered, eyeing the vampire sideways, her eyes full of alarm. "I think they're stuck together for eternity."

Flustered, May looked at Lady Howard, bit her lip, and then leaned back to peer at the vampire again, who was still floating in their general direction, but coolly, slowly. Her mind spun frantically. Finally she looked at the others and then motioned with her bow. "Get in!" she whispered.

For a moment they all looked at her like she'd lost her mind. And then they were piling in on top of the Lady, amid *ows* and *oohs* and whispered *mama mias*. By the time May swooped Kitty from the street and climbed inside, Fabbio was sitting on Lady Howard's lap and Beatrice was stuck against the door so tight she looked to be shrinking. May squeezed in next to Lucius, at which time Pumpkin cleared his throat loudly, stood up, and squeezed between them, wrapping his arms around hers tightly and giving Lucius a superior look. Kitty leaped out of May's arms to get some air at the opposite window.

May had to lean around Pumpkin's big head to get close to the window where the invisible driver sat; again she pointed her silver arrows. Bea grabbed her arm.

"Give instructions wisely," she whispered. "This carriage won't stop once it starts."

May gazed at her and nodded. There was a good chance that the place they were headed had been destroyed, like almost everything else in the Ever After. But what else could they do? May took a deep breath, deciding. "The Scrap Mountains," she commanded. The carriage lurched into motion at breathtaking speed.

"Reeoow," Kitty howled. In a moment of rare gracelessness, he tumbled forward and then, before anyone knew what was happening, straight out the window.

"Kitty!" May lunged forward. "Stop!"

But the carriage didn't stop. May leaped for the doors, one after the other, but both were locked tight. She tried to push her way out of her window, but her shoulders wouldn't fit. All the occupants of the carriage could do was press up against the window to see the scene unfolding behind them: Somber Kitty landing right in the middle of the street and right at the feet of the vampire.

It all happened so quickly it almost seemed like a dream. Kitty looked up at the vampire and let out an innocent "Meow?" The next moment he was swept under the black cape. Smoothly, as if nothing had happened, the vampire turned back from whence he'd come and disappeared into the fog. It was as if neither he nor Kitty had ever been there at all.

"Stop!" May yelled, feeling the world tumble apart inside. "Stop!"

But the carriage kept going, its pace only quickening, until they seemed to be flying down the cobblestone streets.

Lucius took her elbow gently and rested his head against her shoulder. May stretched her arms out the window in a gesture of helplessness.

But it didn't make any difference. Portotown fell away behind them, engulfed in moonlight and fog.

Chapter Nineteen

A Wild Ride

They rode for hours, at times coming within throwing distance of the north end of the Dead Sea, oozing out in front of them slickly, and then they turned north, and for a long time they saw nothing but flat land. May sat staring out the back window, devastated. Beatrice had linked her arm gently through hers, comfortingly, and from time to time May squeezed her hand. After a long bout of hysterical tears, Pumpkin had fallen asleep and was lounging like a rag doll across both of their laps, snoring.

"Ow," Fabbio squealed, jumping up into a crouch. "Madame, I a beg you."

He looked around at the others' bewildered faces, then thrust one finger defensively in the Lady's direction. "She keeps to pincha my behind."

Everyone looked at Lady Howard, who only stared at him mutely, her eyes murderous, her blue lips pursed.

Fabbio twirled his mustache thoughtfully, then reluctantly sat back down on her lap, only to leap up again a few minutes later. "*Lady* Howard, you should be ashamed." But he was blushing a little, and a tiny smile was tucked under his mustache.

Finally they could be seen out the left-hand window—great piles of junk towering out of the emptiness of the Platte in chaotic, grungy lumps. Everyone fell silent.

Beatrice pressed her face against the window, her hands clenched tightly in her lap as she stared. The mountains' inhabitants, the Colony of the Undead, had once helped May and her friends when they needed it most. But there was no telling if they, like so much of the Ever After, had been taken away, Bea's mother among them.

And though no one said it, there was no telling that, if they were there, they would welcome May back. The last time she had seen them, they'd been under the impression she was going to save the realm. And that time, she had only run away.

The carriage lurched to a sudden halt. The doors flew open and everyone tumbled out, landing on the sand. Gathering themselves, they helped one another up, dazed.

Here, all was quiet and still. There was no more moon, only a clear sky with zipping stars, the likes of which May hadn't seen since she'd returned to the Ever After. She gazed up, amazed, and then turned in the direction of Portotown.

"Kitty will find his way back to us," Lucius said. "He will."

May stared into the distance. Kitty was probably more capable of taking care of himself than any of them, that much was true. But still, May's heart was dark with fear for him. If they turned right around and went back to Portotown . . .

"Heeeeeaaaahhhh!"

The yell had issued from Lady Howard's twisted mouth. In a moment the carriage was off again, throwing up a cloud of dust behind it, racing on toward the edge of the realm. They watched it go, then looked at one another. The best thing they could do for Kitty now was to move forward.

"We'd better be quiet," May whispered. If the inhabitants of the Scrap Mountains were here, they might take them for ghouls and . . .

"Wow, you look awful," Pumpkin said, swiping at a few stray tears and taking May in for the first time. Her black velvet dress had ripped in the scuffle at the carriage. Her hair, dirty and moppy from the desert dust, scraggled down her back in crusty lumps, parted only by her arrows.

"Pumpkin, keep your voice down," Bea whispered.

But Pumpkin only shook his head at May in wonder. "Like some kind of . . . nightmare . . . prom queen. . . ."

"Shhh."

They drifted toward the mountain nearest to them. As they got closer, they saw that it was piled with old cars, coffins, and refrigerators. May took in the vast array of junk—including hundreds of hearses, which littered the sand, half-buried—and was disheartened. "I didn't remember there were so many." One of them held an entrance to the Colony, but she had no idea which one.

She looked at Lucius, who glowed like a firefly in the dim emptiness of the desert. He looked back at her and shrugged, as if to say, *Your guess is as good as mine.* Bea, who was trembling, reached for her hand. May held it tight.

"Ooh, shiny," Pumpkin said, reaching out to the pile and grabbing a shiny silver toaster. A tower of hubcaps came cascading down on top of him.

At that moment, just in front of them, there was a crack,

and a shimmying sound, and a slant of warm light shot out across the sand and bathed them in its yellow glow. It wasn't a dim, ghostly glow, but real, living candlelight. The crack widened into a rectangular doorway. The figure that stood within it didn't glow, or float. It was full, solid, colorful, and alive.

Her silhouette was slim and lithe; she wore a black cancan skirt and a red bustier, and her hair was coiffed in a silky brown bob. She held a dagger—pulled from the holster at her thigh—high in the air, threateningly.

Lawless Lexy looked May up and down once, and May wondered if she'd recognize her. And then Lexy sank on one hip, dropping her dagger to her side, and leaned against the doorway.

"Well, well, well, as I live and breathe." Her sharp stare, which never missed a trick, made May squirm.

"We need your help."

Lexy only stood there expectantly.

"We need to send out a message to every group of spirits still left in the Ever After, and to the Lady of North Farm," May said. "We need to get ready to go after Bo Cleevil. Can you help us?"

And then, to May's surprise, Lexy stepped forward and wrapped her in a deep, tight hug, pulling her in through the doorway that led to the Colony of the Undead. "I *love* your hair."

There are many things cats resent. Water, for one. Being scratched in the wrong place, for another. But the one thing cats resent most of all is being held when they don't wish to be. That is why a group of phantoms floating home from Crawl-Mart one evening, their arms full of new daisy-patterned pillow shams, saw a curious thing. A vampire zipping to and fro along the edges of the Platte of Despair, screaming pitifully, a ball of fuzz wrapped around his head like a pair of earmuffs, hanging on for dear life by the teeth.

Apparently, vampires liked biting much more than being bitten.

When Somber Kitty was certain he had gotten his message across, he let go, flying across the air and landing easily on all fours. Tail flapping, he watched as the vampire escaped into the fog. Then he gave his paws a good lick and looked around. He had no idea where he was. It looked more desolate than any spot in the Ever After he had seen—full of drifting fog and emptiness. Somber Kitty let out a purr, gave the ground a good sniff, peered into the fog, picked a direction, and sauntered forward.

He hadn't gotten very far when he saw it. A door, standing in the middle of nothing. He pranced up close, sensing that he shouldn't linger but unable to resist. The door was etched with a skull and crossbones, only the skull was that of an animal—it was horse-shaped, in fact. "Mew?" he asked curiously. It wasn't every day you ran across a drawing of a horse skull in a dead world where all animals were banished. And this door had a smaller square etched in the bottom, right beneath the skull. A *cat* door.

Somber Kitty, who was nearly perfect, did have his flaws, and one of them was conceit. He was sure that whatever danger he was sensing wasn't anything he couldn't handle. He decided to give the door a closer sniff.

He tiptoed forward, his nose quivering, searching. And then, with a great creak, the cat door swung open and a hoof-tipped leg appeared, shooting out around Kitty and scooping him inside.

Chapter Twenty

A Big Nothing

The next night the Colony did something it hadn't done in years. It threw a party.

The cavernous main hall—which opened onto several tunnels that snaked upward through the piles of junk like ant burrows—was festooned with torches dangling from the old chandeliers and tucked into crevices amid the old car parts and coffins piled up to make the walls. Everyone dressed in their finest, which for living outlaws in the land of the dead was their least dirty set of rags. Beatrice and her mother, inseparable since the moment they'd arrived, served refreshments. May, the guest of honor, sat in a corner of the room, watching the others celebrate. Lawless Lexy herself had done her hair, tying it into great and elegant silky knots behind her head and lacing it with flowers from the Colony's gardens. She had dressed May in a fuschia kimono she'd been saving for a rainy day—one she'd had in her trunk the day her ship had gone down in the West Indies. May felt awkward and grown-up.

People kept coming over and pinching her for luck.

"Finally back to finish the job!"

"You're our good luck charm!"

"We knew *The Book of the Dead* wouldn't lie!"

May smiled and nodded painfully. But the truth was, she didn't have a clue what to do next, or if there was anything she *could* do. Anxiously, she turned her mind to Somber Kitty. If anything happened to him, if Bo Cleevil so much as touched a piece of fuzz on his head, she would . . . she would . . .

May, restless, kicked her feet against the sandy floor of the cavern.

"You look like a caged tiger."

May started and turned. Lucius was standing there, his blond hair combed sideways across his forehead, his maroon school jacket freshly pressed, his pinkish cheeks glowing.

"Who did that to your hair?" Lucius asked.

May turned her profile to him, not a little proudly. "Lawless Lexy."

Lucius strung his slingshot and stretched it over and over, gazing about the room. May stared at her fingernails, then at the walls. He kept peeking at her out of the corner of his eye, and May felt herself blushing, feeling pretty. Finally he muttered, "It looks goofy."

May's heart sank. "Well, it's a good thing I don't care what you think," she answered brightly, gazing at a group across the room playing Mother May I. Pumpkin, the farthest behind, kept glancing over at them and narrowing his big black eyes. Lucius shrugged insouciantly and zipped off to find some way to torment the players.

Pumpkin broke policy and did some singing with a backup band of a lesser caliber than he was used to: two banjo pickers and a jug blower. They plucked along merrily through such lounge favorites as "I Left My Hand in Vile Vista" and "You Ain't Nothin' But a Shuck Dog" while the Live Ones danced jigs, or stood along the walls talking and laughing, or sat at the wooden picnic tables swapping tall tales. They played pin the tail on the donkey, musical chairs, all the old favorites from Earth. Beatrice refused to play ring-around-the-rosy because she said it reminded her of the plague, but she taught everyone how to fold handkerchiefs properly.

Bertha, May, and the gang sat at a table in the corner into the wee hours, catching up. Bertha "Bad Breath" Brettwaller may have been the smelliest, but she was also the fiercest and fieriest leader in the Ever After. She leaned forward, cockeyed. "And you haven't received any messages from the Lady since you've been here?"

May shook her head.

Bertha let out a long breath, sending everyone leaning backward. "Curious, that. Very strange indeed."

They watched the band, both lost in their own thoughts. Beatrice was dancing with Fabbio, spinning and spinning.

Lexy appeared, waving a handful of telep-a-grams.

"We've got the first responses back," she said, grinning, and handing them to May.

"That was fast," said May; she had sent out the telep-a-grams that morning, to every place in the realm she could think of. She smiled hopefully at the others.

"Well." Bertha nodded, yanking at her wiry gray hair. "Open 'em!"

May scanned them first for one from the Lady, but nothing. She thought of Bo Cleevil's words. *I'm afraid she's no longer here.* What had he meant? Had she been at the party?

"She'll be in touch when it's time," Bertha said reassuringly.

May opened them one by one—New Egypt, Horrific Hamburgers in the Pit of Despair, the Catacombs. They all looked on eagerly. Then, slowly, their expressions sank as they read the responses.

No thanks, busy that weekend.

Have a dentist appointment.

You must be out of your mind.

There was no word at all from the spirits of Risk Falls.

"Maybe Zero doesn't know how to read," Bea suggested hopefully. Zero was the leader of the wild spirits of Risk Falls.

Bertha sniffed. "Cowards, every one of 'em." She let out a ragged, garlicky sigh, and May and Beatrice exchanged a suffering look. "We've been fighting our tails off," she said, looking tired. "But them dark spirits are like lice, you can't even count 'em there are so many, and there are so few of us. . . ." Bertha shook her shaggy head. "The long and short of it is, they"—Bertha nodded at the responses—"what's left of 'em, they think it's hopeless. The dead aren't very good at hoping, or seeing how things could be different, ya swannee?"

May knew too well the truth of Bertha's words. She had met too many spirits who thought fighting Bo Cleevil was someone else's problem.

Bertha looked at her, cockeyed. "Are you sure you're not just half-dead?" Word had spread quickly of May's fatal tumble off the roof of White Moss Manor. It had been hard for the undead to overcome their glee at May's arrival long enough to express their sympathy. But now Bertha looked at her sadly.

May leaned forward on her elbows. "Pretty sure."

She must have looked especially lost, because Bertha patted her hand with her own rough, calloused one. "Don't you worry. Them astronauts will come for us all one day." Lexy, sitting at Bertha's side, rolled her eyes at May secretly. Ever since May had told Bertha that space travel had been invented, Bertha had been convinced that Earth was working furiously to make contact with the spirit world. Nobody had the heart to burst her bubble.

They all sat silently for several minutes. May looked around at the Colony of the Undead: their careworn, grimy faces, their tattered clothes from years of hiding out in the world of spirits.

"Oh, I can't stand these long faces. Come with me," Bertha ordered.

She summoned them with a nod and they wound their way out of the hall, up through the booby-trapped hallways carved through the garbage. The Colony of the Undead was rigged from top to bottom with traps—set for all manner of dark spirits should they ever be discovered—that only the undead knew about. Bertha carefully steered them around, over, and under them, and up. "It's probably the safest place in the realm now," she said, "aside from North Farm." The roof gave them a view of the surrounding desert.

May had stood here once before, when Kitty was still by her side, when she had been sure of the Lady, when things in the Ever After had seemed so scary. It hadn't been nearly as scary as now.

"The Galaxy Gulf's a nice place to see," Bertha said, pointing off north. "Lots of exciting things to visit, even out here in the Nothing Platte. Well, used to be that way. Now it's just empty Cleevilvilles, and anyone who's left doesn't dare go out."

Staring across the sandy platte, May gasped. In the air, a giant shadow was moving across the sand far away, back and forth. May could just make out that it had the shape of a hand, a hand that looked like it was feeling around on a dark shelf.

"Bo Cleevil's looking for you, all right," said Bertha.

May watched the giant shadow hand.

"Bertha, what is Bo Cleevil, exactly? I mean, what kind of spirit is he?"

"He's more powerful than you've seen yet, my dear. And none of us can hide from him forever." Bertha nodded ominously toward the giant, shadowy hand. "He'll find us eventually."

A deep shadow settled over May's heart.

"I have to go see the Lady," she said.

"Girly, now you know that if the Lady hasn't invited you, you'll never make it across the Petrified Pass. Remember what happened last time?"

May thought of the terrors that had awaited them in the tunnels beneath the Petrified Pass, where they had faced their worst fears.

"Achoo!" Everyone standing around Bertha leaned back as she snuffled and let out a big, stinky breath. "The Lady works in her own time. If she wants you, she'll call you. Meanwhile, we gotta wait for her before we can do anything about Bo

Cleevil. I don't think we can succeed without her." She nodded to the shadow hand. "As long as there's still a little light left in the Ever After, we have time. And there'll be light in the Ever After until the very last town has fallen."

May kicked at the ground darkly. "But we can't just *sit* here in the meantime."

"I suggest . . ." Fabbio paused dramatically, then whispered, "Sabotage." He thrust a finger in the air grandly.

"How do you sabotage the world's most powerful dark spirit?" May asked.

"Bo Cleevil's biggest thing is fear. What's our biggest thing?" Beatrice asked logically. Her hands were busy folding her sash into exact right triangles.

May looked around the group. Pumpkin was patting his tuft and intoning low *me-me-me-me-meee*'s. Beatrice had moved on to cleaning her fingernails with a special brush she'd found down below. Lucius was making farting noises with his hands, right near Fabbio's rear, and then pulling away quickly. Fabbio kept looking behind him, bewildered, and then around at the group, blushing.

"Goofiness?" May said despondently.

Lucius floated upright, a rakish grin spreading across his lips. His glow had multiplied so exponentially that everyone had to squint, surprised, to look at him. May lifted her hands over her eyes to soften the glare. "What are you thinking?" she asked.

·

Chapter Twenty-one

The Free Spirits Were Here

Snicker, snicker, snicker.

Flapping his tail, Somber Kitty stared up at the spirit who had accosted him. His captor looked to be having quite a laugh, blowing air through his great nostrils, his big lips almost smiling. The great animal nudged Kitty, as if wanting to play, and let out a whinny. Horses could be so immature.

Somber Kitty peered around, taking in the scene before him. Rolling hills, full of tigers, snakes, bats, cats, armadillos, anteaters, three-toed sloths, dodo birds, dogs . . . every animal in the rainbow loped across the green grass, flew through the blue sky, frolicked amongst the trees. Somber Kitty was no detective, but something told him this was the realm to which all animal spirits had been banished. And something told him they weren't having all that bad of a time.

Somber Kitty gave his whiskers a twitch, stood up, and gave the horse a parting wave of his tail. It was all very lovely, but he had other things to do. Mainly, he had a girl he needed to protect.

He was just turning to leave when he saw her.

She was gray, in a purple collar. Her delicate paws were

wrapped around a twig, which she was gnawing on ecstatically while writhing back and forth on her back. She seemed to sense she was being watched, for her ears turned to Kitty, and then the rest of her did, and she bounced into the air like a Super Ball and landed on all fours, looking at him. Trying to look as smooth as possible, Somber Kitty lay down on his belly and belly-crawled toward her.

"Meow," he said, which in English means, "Hey babe, I have somewhere I need to be, wanna come with?"

"Mew," she replied, which in English means, "Love to."

And, far from being trapped, the two cats simply traipsed out the way Somber Kitty had come.

THE PLATTE OF DESPAIR MEDITATION
AND YOGA RETREAT FOR BUSY GOBLINS.

May, Lucius, Pumpkin, and Beatrice stood with their backs against a red brick wall on which these words were announced, staring across the lawn at something they had written in the grass.

They couldn't help but admire what they'd done.

"Do you think we should add some curlicues?" Bea asked. "It could be dressed up a bit." Lucius and May blinked at each other, shaking their heads. Fabbio had stayed home to play badminton, considering the whole outing useless. Staring at what they'd just done to the lawn of the Yoga Retreat, May thought he might have a point.

"Well," she breathed, "let's go."

They sneaked into the building through the side door, first

going into the locker room. Through a window they could see several goblins sitting in lotus position in the room beyond, their eyes closed.

On the far wall was a sign:

MANTRA: WHEN I GET TIRED OF TERRORIZING OTHERS,
THERE IS A PLACE I CAN GO TO RECHARGE.

They rolled their eyes at one another, and then sneaked onward, arriving at a room where the goblins had hung their slimy clothes. Lucius opened a couple of the washing machines and began mixing lights and darks. Beatrice went to work, putting glops of ectoplasm in the rows of designer shoes, grimacing at the slimy goo. Pumpkin hovered near the door, nibbling his long white fingers and ready to escape at any moment. May found a stash of shoe polish and hurried to the showers to mix it up with the goblins' shampoo.

While she was busy with that, Lucius drifted past, holding his nose and wincing, his arms full of underwear. Noticing May's boggled look, he motioned for her to follow him to the kitchen, then to a giant silver refrigerator against the far wall. The room was lined with kegs labeled ORGANIC GUTT-GRASS JUICE. "Can you open the freezer for me?" Lucius whispered.

May had to cover her mouth to keep from laughing as they shoved pile after pile of goblin underwear into the freezer.

Lucius waved a pair of underwear at her threateningly.

She waggled another pair back at him. They burst into an underwear sword fight, dodging left and right, cutting capers, waving the underwear behind their backs and through their legs, dashing at each other like swordsmen.

"Fear the undies," Lucius growled.

"Never!" May hissed back, throwing her underwear so that it landed square on his head.

"Really, you two." They both turned to see Beatrice in the doorway, frowning sternly. "If the goblins catch us . . ."

Pumpkin was standing by one of the Organic Guttgrass Juice urns, trying to pour himself a glass. He kept tilting the urn farther forward, finally sticking his mouth under the tap. The three turned to watch him and realized a moment too late what was about to happen.

The urn reached its tipping point. And suddenly it came crashing down, dousing Pumpkin in green glowing juice and rolling across the floor.

A moment later a figure appeared behind Bea in the doorway. May and Lucius noticed it first and then, seeing their eyes, Beatrice's own widened in fright and she swiveled, coming face-to-face with a fearsome goblin, about half her size but with razor-sharp teeth that took up almost his entire face. He was wearing a turban and ballet pants.

"Ahh!"

They all turned and ran for the back kitchen door—knocking aside big kegs of Organic Guttgrass Juice in their wake—and burst onto the front lawn, zipping off into the night, laughing madly.

Behind them they left a chaotic scene of goblins screaming and screeching to find their lights and darks had all turned the same shade of pink, and a reminder blazing on the front lawn:

THE FREE SPIRITS WERE HERE!

"That underwear idea of mine was *good*," Lucius said, grinning from ear to ear. He picked a nightshade flower that happened to be growing near where his feet landed and handed it to May. Pumpkin let out a tiny growl, almost like he was clearing his throat. May took the flower and twined it about her bowstring, looking at Pumpkin curiously, then back at Lucius.

"Yeah, it was," she said, like a mother would say to a child, exchanging a grin with Beatrice.

"I outdo myself sometimes," he said, reaching down for another flower and handing it back to her. This one May tucked behind her ear. A moment later Pumpkin's long white hand appeared at the corner of her eye as he plucked the flower from her ear and tucked it behind his own, scowling at Lucius's back.

"I'm glad you died at thirteen, May. Now we'll be the same age forever."

Pumpkin wagged his head back and forth and made kissy faces at May behind Lucius's back. May gave him a pinch.

"I'm not so sure *I'm* glad," May said, shooting Lucius a significant look, but he appeared oblivious, smiling to himself.

Beatrice squeezed May's hand and smiled sympathetically. "I nearly swooned when I saw that goblin!" she breathed.

"Race you to the abandoned hearse," Lucius said, punching May's arm and zipping past. She gave chase, feeling utterly free. She was the first to slam her hand on the hearse, and Lucius collapsed on the sand, grinning. Unlike the boys at Hog Wallow Middle, he looked happy that May had won.

"Faster than a speeding bullet!" he said. Pumpkin drifted past them and on to the Colony, his nose up in the air. Bea drifted along behind him, no doubt off to do laundry.

May rushed to catch up, eager to see if they'd received any message from the Lady.

Any day now she would send for them.

Any day, they'd know why it was taking her so long.

Two cats—one fluffy and gray, one hairless and rather ugly—slowly made their way west across the Nothing Platte.

Somber Kitty's companion had introduced herself as Mew, which Somber Kitty interpreted as "Pretty Fluffy Face." While he stalked along the sand seriously, she zipped in circles around him, tackling him by the neck, nibbling on his ears, and generally trying to remind him to lighten up.

However, they both had the same reaction when they came upon a stone structure buried in the sand. Its crooked and sunken doorway was strung with cobwebs, concealing the darkness within. It seemed to shout that here lay certain danger. If either of them had been familiar with Egyptology, they would have recognized it for what it was—an ancient tomb.

It looked so unquestionably forbidding that the cats, with one look at each other, padded up for a closer look. Tails stiff and ears swiveling like satellites, they traipsed down the stairs into the darkness, full of delight.

Somewhere far below, in the belly of the tomb, there was a groan. They hurried forward to investigate.

Chapter Twenty-two

Meatballs of Fire

May sat with her chin in her hand, staring out the window at thousands of hot fiery balls zooming out of the sky and landing with great *thwack*s across the Nothing Platte, sending up clouds of sand and fire in the dark as far as the eye could see.

For two weeks they'd been playing pranks all over the northern realm. But they'd been trapped inside for the past three days.

"It's meteor-showering cats and dogs," Beatrice said with a sigh. They were all lounging in May's room, a circular, cave-like affair tucked up in one of the high corners of the Scrap Mountains, with a breathtaking view of the Platte. Beatrice sat perched on the arm of May's moldy, busted easy chair, braiding May's long hair over and over. Lucius lay on the floor, his hands beneath his head, wiggling his heels restlessly. Fabbio sat on the edge of May's bed, composing a poem he had announced was called "Meatballs of Fire."

"Yeah," May murmured, thinking of Somber Kitty. She hadn't known there were such things as meteor showers in the Ever After, but apparently there were, and apparently it was very dangerous to go out in them unless you had a really good umbrella. She hoped Kitty was somewhere safe.

"Woo-hoo!"

The sound had come from down the hall. A moment later Pumpkin appeared, carrying a newspaper in his hands. "Look what just came in the telep-a-booth! We're famous!"

"Let's see it, Pumpkin." Lucius reached out for the paper. But Pumpkin held it back and gave Lucius a sniffy look.

"May and I would like to look at it first," he said, looking Lucius up and down, then grabbing May by the shroud and pulling her aside so they could lean over the paper. "I wonder what I'll get famous for next," Pumpkin said.

Wave of Banditry Strikes Northeast

Ghouls, goblins, and zombies in the northeastern territories were disturbed by a rash of bizarre incidents this week. Sometime in the wee hours of Tuesday night, a giant billboard of Bo Cleevil, the realm's ruler, was vandalized—as discovered the following morning by a group of goblins returning from the Glammy Guts Mall in Grief Glenn. The vandals had drawn a curly mustache on the obscured face of Bo Cleevil, along with boogers coming out of his nose.

In Upper Transylvania on Wednesday, a twelve-pack of Slurpy Soda cans exploded when a pack of ghouls tried to drink them. Later that afternoon, the same ghouls found YOU SMELL painted across their windshield. Arguments have since broken out about exactly which ghoul the YOU SMELL was directed at, and what exactly they are alleged to smell like.

And on Thursday, a horde of zombies was stopped dead in its tracks when a tall man in a curly mustache began dancing in front of them, singing "That's Amore." Some hobgoblins tried to give chase, only to find that their shoelaces had been tied together. They lay helpless for several hours while waiting for someone to arrive who knew how to untie shoes.

On a more serious note, countless spears and arrows have been reported missing from the Grim Reaper Supply Shop outside the shattered remains of Hocus Pocus.

Several specters we interviewed Friday outside Glammy Guts claimed to be "amused" by the pranks, and anonymous guillotined sources in Portotown, fearless of losing their heads because they already have, say that it's about time somebody in the Ever After showed a little chutzpah.

No matter who the pranksters are, or what their motivations might be, spirits all over the realm have begun to look to the northeast with anticipation, wondering what may happen next.

"It's brought a little light into our afterlives," one anonymous spirit said, "knowing that someone is out there, bucking the system."

Someone, indeed. But who?

Fabbio stood up and, seeming suddenly inspired, zipped off down the hallway.

"I told you we were good," Lucius said, folding his hands behind his head.

May turned to look out the window again at the meteor shower. "I don't know."

"What's not to know?" Pumpkin said, flopping onto the arm of May's chair and swinging his legs. "The truth is, I just can't not be famous no matter how hard I try."

May couldn't help feeling annoyed at Pumpkin. Seeing his glee, and Lucius's self-congratulatory smile, she felt like she was the only one in the room who remembered why they were here in the first place. Only Beatrice seemed to be listening seriously.

"Go on, May, what do you mean?" she asked, leaning forward.

"Well, we've just pulled some pranks. That's all. We haven't saved anybody. We haven't done anything important."

Beatrice nodded. "Yes, I suppose it *sounds* that way. But look, it says right here we're making a difference. Here, the part about bringing light into their afterlifes . . ."

"But that won't save Somber Kitty," May argued, frustrated. "Or save the realm, or—"

She was interrupted by the curious sight of Fabbio rushing back through the doorway, his arms full of papers. He dumped them onto May's lap.

"I'm thinking now that we are famous it is time."

"Time for what?" May asked, gazing at the papers, confused.

"Time to submit some of my work to be published. You see," he said, shuffling through his papers, "poems, screenplays, novels. I do it all. I shall read you one of my poems now. It is called 'I Am So Talented I Make Myself Cry."

"Ooh . . . ," Pumpkin cooed, picking up a screenplay titled, in glowing letters across the front, *Stone Toe: An Autobiography*. "Have you started casting for this yet?" A delighted smile came over his face.

"You should cast me," Lucius said, standing up and puffing out his chest. "Did you see me when those ghouls were chasing us? Quick as a flash. Tough as . . ." His blue eyes sparkled. "Something really tough." He grinned proudly. Beatrice laughed and clapped.

May felt her impatience reach a fever pitch. She stood up, dumping Fabbio's papers off her lap, and reached for her bow and quiver.

Everyone stopped in the middle of what they were doing to look at her.

"Where are you off to all of a sudden?" Lucius asked, the grin still playing on his lips.

"We're not gonna get anything done without the Lady," May said, slinging the quiver over her back in a passion. "I'm going to get her."

"But May," Beatrice insisted, "the Petrified Pass. Bertha said—"

"Something could happen to you." It was Pumpkin who'd spoken, his fingers in his mouth, suddenly as worried as he'd been delighted a moment before. But it was too late. May was too angry to stop being angry.

"Why don't you go back to reading *Stone Toe*," May spat. "Since all you care about is being famous."

"Hey, that's uncalled-for," Lucius interrupted, but May ignored him. She was impossibly angry at Pumpkin, and she didn't even know why. Maybe it was because he didn't argue with her. He only looked shattered.

"I'll come with you," he offered finally.

His kindness filled her with shame, and that only made her angrier. "You're the one who always gets us caught, Pumpkin. I'm safer without you."

As soon as the words were out, May wished for all the world she could take them back. Pumpkin looked down at his fingers, his white cheeks turning rosy red.

The others stared, mouths agape. Fabbio cleared his throat. Bea tugged at her sash. Lucius glowered. But it couldn't make May feel worse than she already did. She turned to leave.

"May, please don't go," Beatrice said.

"I'm dead anyway," she shot back. "What's the worst that could happen?"

Seconds later she was charging out into the storm.

Somber Kitty and the cat known as Pretty Fluffy Face knew they'd made a mistake the minute they noticed that the groaning, which heretofore had been somewhere up ahead in the darkness, began to come from directly behind them and then, a moment later, all around them.

They scanned the darkness of the tomb with their keen eyes, seeing nothing but walls. And then they saw the movement—figures that at first had seemed to be only paintings detaching themselves from the walls, their arms held aloft, reaching, grasping.

The mummies lurched toward the cats, closing in on them from all sides.

Somber Kitty leaped in front of Pretty Fluffy Face and let out a low growl, his tail standing warningly. As one mummy hand reached for him, he bit it as hard as he could, but the hand only reached around his middle and grasped him tight.

Somber Kitty tried to leap away, pulling at the mummy's gauze as he did. It came away in his teeth—a long thread unraveling from around the mummy's thumb, leaving nothing behind. Where the thumb had been a moment before, there was only thin air.

Somber Kitty looked down at Pretty Fluffy Face, who was watching raptly as two mummies crept up behind her. The circle of mummies grew tighter, closing in, until the cats lost sight of each other completely.

Chapter Twenty-three

Back to North Farm

That night, not long after she left, May—after having dodged her way across the Nothing Platte, nearly being squashed by several meteors—found a cave in which to take shelter. She curled up in the ratty blanket she'd brought and watched the meteors fall, the fires bathing her face in a warm glow. She seethed with shame. She kept thinking of Pumpkin's face when she had said the things she had. She kept thinking of how worried they all must be about her, and how terrible she had probably made them feel.

After a long while, May unfurled herself onto her back, staring at the darkness of the cave ceiling above. She remembered nights lying awake in her bed back home, studying the ceiling, the sound of the TV down the hall, the comforting knowledge that her mom was there, still awake.

Did some souls really lose the place they belonged to? Had Bo Cleevil been right?

May certainly felt lost in space.

She hoped that, like the last time, the Lady could show her the way.

· · ·

The following day May trekked across the rocky lowlands for seemingly endless hours. She found herself humming one of Pumpkin's silly songs, then thinking of Fabbio's poetry and wishing she could hear some of it, terrible as it was. She kept her eyes trained on the shadowy mountains ahead, which seemed like they'd never get any closer.

But finally the land began to rise, and up ahead she could see the dim evening light glinting off the giant bones that littered the Petrified Pass. After another hour or so she approached the giant stone that marked the edge of the pass. It was broken in two, the engraved words on its surface sliced down the middle:

HERE LIE THE FROST GIANTS

AND HERE THEY STOOD

THEY WERE BELIEVED INTO LIFE

AND THEN FORGOTTEN.

NOW ONLY THEIR LONELY BREATH

DRIFTS UPON THE MOUNTAINS

AND GUARDS THE WAY WITH FEAR.

May looked up into the snowy mountains, crossing her arms over herself. And then she realized that she wasn't cold at all. The frigid breath of the mountains that had so shrouded her and her friends the last time they had come no longer affected her. The bones of the giants, which had so terrified them, now looked pitiful and defeated where they lay strewn across the rocky hills, though May couldn't exactly put her finger on why.

Something wasn't right. She looked back over her shoulder, stroking her long black ponytail thoughtfully, wondering if maybe it had been a mistake to come after all. But she couldn't face going back to the Colony empty-handed. She set her chin and pushed onward.

She spent that night camped in a nook about two hours' distance from the top of the rise, watching for ghost lights dancing amongst the shadows but seeing nothing except the dark. She tried to ignore the unease that enveloped her. There was no sign of the tunnels they'd stumbled into before. The mountain was lifeless and still.

Her fears were confirmed when she crested the rise late the next morning. What she saw on the other side made her ghostly heart stand still.

In the valley below, where there had once been a primeval forest, its canopy dusted with snow but brimming with life underneath, lay a graveyard of chopped and decayed wood. Not a tree had been left standing. The tangled vines and fireflies and filmy animals and glowing North Farm spirits were gone. Now May drifted down into the valley slowly, as if in a dream.

She drifted past the sign, now crooked and cracked, announcing WILD AND WOOLLY NORTH FARM, into what had been the heart of North Farm. All around her was evidence of its previous inhabitants—fine spinning looms, whetting stones, and forges, all the things the spirits had used to make the finest hand-crafted products in the Ever After.

And then she came to a great tangle of roots, ten stories high or more, and gasped. It was the Lady's magnolia tree. May crawled over and around each limb, getting covered with mud, searching for something the Lady may have left, some sign that she might be somewhere, might still be all right. There was nothing—just the Lady's old photos, a broken table where they had once sat together, a handful of red magnolia seeds, and a glowing sign, sticking up from the dirt.

COMING SOON!
CLEEVILRAMA MALL AND MULTIPLEX
EIGHTEEN-SCREEN THEATER WITH SPECIAL GOBLIN SEATING!
THREE HUNDRED STORES TO CHOOSE FROM,
ALL SELLING MOSTLY THE SAME THINGS!
TREE MUSEUM! POLTERGEIST AQUARIUM! FOOD COURT!

May sank onto one of the limbs, her strength disappearing. A stray lightning bug flitted across her vision. She watched it buzz away.

She didn't know how long she sat there. But finally she stood up, ran her hands through her hair, then stuck her hands in her pockets. She wished there were something for her to bring back to the Colony of the Undead. But there was nothing left of the heart of the Ever After.

In the desert, one last groaning voice issued from deep within a buried tomb and then went silent. Sand blew across the tomb door, shaking the cobwebs. All went back to how it had been, as if nothing had happened there at all.

Chapter Twenty-four

Galaxy Gulf

May's mind was full of many things, and she was hardly aware she was drifting at all.

After hours of wandering, she found herself at the edge of what must be the Galaxy Gulf. It looked like the Grand Canyon, only instead of a bottom there was endless space.

May stood at the edge, kicking some sand and watching it plummet down into the emptiness. Why did it have to be her, standing here with the weight of the world on her shoulders? Why couldn't she be Claire Arneson, comfy in her bed? Why couldn't she be just an average skulldog vendor in Stabby Eye? Why couldn't she be the old May, who never knew there was so much danger in the world?

She ran her hands through her hair, the fingers of her right hand happening to brush something stuck there. She pulled it out and sat down, swinging her legs over the edge of the canyon. It was a red magnolia seed. She dropped it beside her.

Finally she stood up. She took one last woozy look down into the depths of the canyon, and then she turned back in the direction she'd come.

A rattling behind her caught her by surprise, and she whipped around.

The seed had sprouted, and before her eyes, in seconds, it grew into a small tree. But the tree swiveled as if to look at her, and May saw that it wasn't a tree at all, but the Lady herself, lined like a piece of old wood.

May stood transfixed, scared to believe what she was seeing. The Lady tree blew in the breeze. Her limbs gestured to May.

"Hi," she said. "Remember me?"

She reached out toward May. She looked so delicate, as if she might break, that May was scared to touch her.

"Oh, I'm not *that* old. Come on, now."

May reached out one hand, and when the Lady's dry, brittle hand touched hers, she knew it was real.

"You look breakable," she breathed.

"I'm always breakable." The Lady sighed. "Sometimes it's just more obvious than others."

"Why didn't you stop them?" May asked. It was the first thing that came into her head.

The Lady looked at her like she'd asked the simplest question in the world. "Why, stopping them's not up to me, my dear."

May's thoughts circled around her head and tied themselves in knots, so that she couldn't say anything in reply.

The Lady seemed unfazed. "Personally, I just like to go with the flow," she said.

May opened and closed her mouth, but she was speechless.

"Wanna see something?" Without waiting for an answer, the Lady reached out her hand and pulled May to the edge of the cliff. She nodded out beyond its edge. "Let's go, then."

May stared at the great emptiness beyond the cliff's edge. "You want me to walk out there?"

The Lady blinked at her for a moment, and then her wrinkled face lit up with recognition. "Oh yes, you're right."

She held out her hand, where a tiny white sticker had materialized. The sticker said HELLO, MY NAME IS and then MAY in glowing, sloppy letters. Above these words, it said GUEST, VIP TOUR OF THE GALAXY.

"Having a proper pass is one of the rules of the universe. You're absolutely right to want to stick to protocol." The Lady smiled. "Well, better hurry up if you want to see. You haven't got much time."

She waved May forward. May peered out over the ledge again, into the great star-filled abyss there. "See what?" she asked.

"Why, everything," the Lady said, looking short on patience, her eyes growing panther-sharp as she reached out her wrinkled hand.

May swallowed. Half regretting it already, she reached out for the Lady's hand. She took a step. And then she was floating on thin air, with nothing underneath her but stars. She felt as light and aimless as a balloon. She smiled a breathless smile.

"Right, then," the Lady said. Her roots trailing behind her like the train of a bridal gown, she too drifted out over the edge. And then they were floating, down into the gulf, down, down, down, and then out underneath it, into open space. May looked behind her. She could see the Ever After—a dim, round sphere of gas behind them.

As they drifted away, it became smaller and smaller.

"Now if you'll look to your left . . ." The Lady behaved

like the perfect tour guide, speaking mechanically, as if she had done it a thousand times. She pointed out supernovas, comets, planets, nebulae, alien truck stops, the best planets to go to for live music, some random bundles of space trash, a few satellites, and several black holes. "Which one's the sun?" May asked, gazing about at all the stars.

The Lady grinned a wooden smile at her. May pictured, for a moment, how odd they would look to someone watching from Earth—a tree and a girl floating through space. "Earth's sun?"

May nodded.

The Lady pointed to a tiny pin dot. May wondered how she could possibly know.

"And which one's the Earth?"

The Lady pointed to another pin dot. It didn't look like anything May knew. It didn't look big enough to hold all the people and animals and feelings that filled it up.

"So tiny. And everyone gets so worked up about things," the Lady said, tsk-tsking.

May nodded. "But there's love there."

"That's true. Love is bigger than it looks."

May stared at the Earth. It was so impossibly far away. Her eyes began to well with tears.

"Now." The Lady frowned and shoved a crisp white hanky into her hand. "No use crying over spilled milk. If you waste your time crying over where you *used* to be, you'll miss all the good things happening around you. Like for instance, a VIP tour of the galaxy. Plus, feeling sorry for yourself never helped anybody. You've done that a great deal too much recently, my dear."

May thought about her poor behavior back at the Colony of the Undead and was filled again with shame. She wondered if Pumpkin would ever forgive her.

They floated past clouds of bright cosmic dust that filled May with wonder, and stars that burned so brightly she had to look away.

They floated for several more minutes. And just when May thought they were millions of light-years from the Ever After, it was looming toward them, getting larger and larger. She could recognize it by the big billboard, proclaiming BO CLEEVIL IS NUMBER ONE, that hovered just in front of it, blinking with a neon glow. The rest of the star was wrapped in shade.

"It's so dark."

"It's lost its heart. It's empty. That's all."

They landed gently, hovering just above the ground. May waited for the Lady to say something, hoping desperately that it wasn't time for good-bye. She had so many questions. She had so much more to say.

"I'm not very good at being a spirit," May said. The Lady smiled. "But I'm not sure I was very good at being a girl, either."

"You were, May. The thing is, if one's going to be alive, one's got to commit to it a hundred percent. Be there all the way. Let it all hang out. All that kind of stuff. Otherwise, what fun is it?"

May had no answer for that. Now that she was stuck in the world of ghosts, she wished she had lived a little more. Been braver. Found where she fit.

"Oh, it's charming, the Ever After. Or it *was*," said the Lady, casting a glance into the gulf. "The Pit of Despair, and the colorful spirits and specters, the comfort of things being the same year after year, all that. But Earth . . ." She sighed. "Earth is special."

Suddenly, from somewhere behind May, there was a giant clap of thunder, and then a gleaming white light. "Oh, it's arrived," the Lady said, as May whirled around.

A bridge stood before her, glowing and covered with fireflies, leading up into the sky. The edge of it disappeared into the darkness above.

"Is that . . ."

"Of course."

May walked up to its edge, her long hair tangling around her neck, reaching out gingerly to touch its railing, then looking at the Lady dubiously.

"Why is it here?" She worried, suddenly, that one of them was going to be taken across.

"I wanted you to see it."

"What's beyond there?"

"I don't know. Nobody has ever come back."

The bridge seemed to stretch right into the dark sky above. And May realized, staring into that darkness, what had intrigued her most about the Bridge of Souls. She looked back over her shoulder at the Lady. "Do you think I would never be afraid there?"

"Yes, yes I do. I think you would never be afraid there."

May looked toward the edge. She reached out her hand again to the railing.

"Seems like a good chance to run away from it all, doesn't it?"

May looked at her. She lifted one foot and put it on the first step of the bridge. She thought for a long time. And then, with a feeling of sadness, she pulled her foot back.

A few minutes later they stood in the dark on the edge of the Nothing Platte, talking quietly.

"You won't stay with us?"

"It isn't my fight. But I'll be around. In my way."

"Do you think I can do it? Do you think I can do what the book said?"

The Lady stared at her a long moment, then sighed. "May, I'm as old as time itself. I don't think, I *know*." She looked torn. "And I hate to be the bearer of bad tidings as much as the next person." Her blue eyes grew wide, deep as pools. "May, you will fail."

May was so stunned, she floated backward.

"How can you say that?"

The Lady shrugged her limbs, looking sympathetic but not crushed. "It's the truth."

"So you're saying I should give up?"

The Lady clucked her tongue and shook her leafy head. "Knowing you will lose is no reason to give up. Dear me. Now, I have a speaking engagement in the Black Eye galaxy and I need to get back to it. So if you'll excuse me . . ."

May wanted to beg the Lady for help. But she didn't. She lifted her chin, trying to look courageous.

The Lady bustled away a few feet, then happened to turn back and, seeing May's expression, seemed to think better of it. She folded her leaves thoughtfully in front of her. "Don't worry, May. There are still a few nice surprises in store for you."

She smiled, as if nothing in the world were wrong at all. And then she crumpled up like dirt and blew away.

Galaxy Gulf was far behind her when the first silhouettes of the Scrap Mountains came into view.

May could see right away that something wasn't quite right. Every window—normally dark with camouflage—was alight with an unmistakable yellow glow. And up on the roof stood a gaggle of ominous-looking figures—not Live Ones, but glowing, ghostly, dead.

She began to run.

Chapter Twenty-five

A Special Delivery

ay had her arrows strung and ready when she burst through the secret door into the main hall of the Colony of the Undead. Her first thought was how many dark spirits there were. Her second thought was that they didn't quite look like dark spirits. Then she realized that they weren't dark spirits at all.

May lowered her arrows, bewildered.

"Nice of you to drop in," Pumpkin said, drifting past with his arm looped through the arm of a specter in a toga.

May peered about. The cavern was full of spirits: a horde of luminous boys gathered in a circle getting instructions from Lucius, several spirits she recognized from Horrific Hamburgers at the Pit of Despair, some ancient Egyptians, ghosts of various shapes and sizes with bulging eyeballs, or horns, or gooey drippy tails, even a handful of North Farm spirits, brightly lit, their cometlike tails drifting behind them as they floated in circles.

"What . . ."

"May!" Beatrice appeared, beaming, and wrapped her in a hug. "Isn't it wonderful?"

May stared at her, dumbfounded.

"They've all come to help. Everyone wants to join the Free Spirits. They said they were inspired, since we've made Bo Cleevil look less fearsome. They've actually started to believe we can win."

May couldn't believe it. A feeling of hope began to flood her soul. She clutched Bea's hands.

CRASH!

At that moment the western wall of the hall came crashing in, junk flying everywhere. Several spirits in the hall screamed. Those who didn't pulled back in shock.

Whatever had come in with the rubble landed in a heap, and a moment later began to move. A gasp went around the room. Hubcaps went spinning across the floor as several figures emerged from the debris: a girl with alligator scars, several boys wearing war paint and feathers in their hair, and one boy in particular, in a pair of colorful tropical shorts, with sparkling eyes and zinc across his nose.

He looked around, nodding, as if satisfied. A bright orange parachute was strapped to his back. He held a square white box, marked with a skull and crossbones and the word SKULLIONI'S, aloft in one hand. Hot, white, delicious-smelling steam poured out from its sides.

"Dudes," Zero said, ruffling his hair casually and shaking it out, "I heard we're saving the world." He nodded gamely. "Who wants pizza?"

The spirits of Risk Falls had arrived.

"When the time comes, we'll reach the Platte of Despair this way," Bertha said, her grimy hands holding a map of the Ever After pinned to the table in the main hall. A small group of spirits, including Lucius, Pumpkin, and Lawless Lexy, sat around, listening raptly. "If . . . once we get to the fortress—," she went on.

"We'll need to wait until the dark spirits start leaving before we do anything," May said, anticipating Bertha's words. For two weeks they had been planning and replanning, thinking and rethinking, their approach to Bo Cleevil's fortress. There were many unknowns. No one knew exactly what the castle was like, even though Beatrice had read everything she could find on the subject. No one knew how exactly they were going to get inside. What they did know was that when Bo Cleevil's grip on the Ever After was complete, he would be sending a host of dark spirits all over the realm, to take up their malicious lives in the Cleevilvilles. And that meant that, while still impossibly strong, his defenses would be weaker than usual. It also meant that the best time to strike was also the time when the Earth would be in the most possible danger.

May hated to wait that long. And as long as Kitty was still out there, her sense of urgency would be double. Being patient was as hard as anything she'd ever done. But she knew it was their only chance.

As the weeks had passed, the numbers of Free Spirits hiding at the Colony had grown. Peering around the main hall, she could see Zero explaining to a group of New Egyptians, some ancient Greeks, and a group of belly dancers how to put a ghoul in a headlock. Fabbio was running a ragtag troop of ghosts through the Undead's obstacle course. Beatrice was teaching a group of Risk Fallsers how to be discreet.

May stood up. "I need to go think for a while," she said, moving to leave.

"I'll come with you," said Lucius.

"*I'll* come with you." Pumpkin leaped from his chair and squeezed between Lucius and May, narrowing his eyes at Lucius. May flashed Lucius an apologetic smile, then floated down the hallway with Pumpkin. Once they got to May's room, she flopped into the rickety easy chair by the window and stared out at the desert thoughtfully. Pumpkin flopped on her bed and started playing finger puppets, making one May and one Lucius.

"I'm sooooo great," he had the Lucius finger puppet say.

"Oohhhh, Lucius, you're so right," the May finger puppet said. "You're totally my hero."

"Pumpkin," May asked, curious, "why are you so mean to Lucius?"

Pumpkin yawned. "You and he seem to be awfully chummy these days," he said, picking invisible lint out of his tuft of hair.

May didn't respond. She guessed they *were* sort of chummy.

"So I guess now *he's* your best friend all of a sudden," Pumpkin went on. May turned to him, surprised.

"Pumpkin, how can you say that?"

Pumpkin frowned at her and dropped his finger puppets into regular hands. "Tell me the truth. Do you like him better than me?"

May didn't know how to explain. "No, of course not. I just like him . . . different." She didn't know how she liked Lucius.

"Hmph," Pumpkin said.

May opened her mouth to say more when a noise from downstairs distracted them both. Giving each other a look, they shot up and hurried through the junk-lined tunnels to the main hall, where a group of specters were gathered in a circle, talking loudly and agitatedly.

"What is it?" May asked, suddenly worried.

Someone shoved a paper into her hands.

"It came in the telep-a-booth," said Lawless Lexy, giving her a grave look. May looked down at the headlines. A picture of a burning mansion flickered on the front page, beneath the headline LAST HAUNT IN THE EVER AFTER KICKS THE BUCKET.

May looked up from the paper, bewildered. "But what does it mean?" she asked.

"It's true. I seen it from up yonder," Bertha growled, stepping out of one of the tunnels and dusting off her boots. "Portotown has fallen." Several spirits around the hall gasped, but Bertha looked only at one person—May. "The realm's last free city is gone."

May drifted up to the doorway to the outdoors and opened it, peering outside as if she might see Portotown crumbling in the distance. There was only empty desert.

Only the faintest glimmer remained in the sky above. The last of the stars above the Nothing Platte had vanished. There was no escaping it: The Ever After was flickering out.

As she was looking, May sensed a movement not too far off across the sand. She started. In a flash she had her arrows drawn, pointing into the darkness.

For several seconds she stood there, straining her ears for the slightest sound. Behind her, the colony prepared itself, spirits racing to and fro for whatever was approaching outside.

They pressed themselves against the walls, poised to fight, listening for the slightest sound that might give away who was outside. And then it came.

"Meay."

May's arrow went clattering to the ground.

She could just make out now, a few feet away, the big ears silhouetted in the starlight. She was just about to leap forward when she froze again. Somber Kitty wasn't the only figure there in the dusk. There were two mummies, their hands tied together by their own gauze, held like a leash that dangled from Somber Kitty's mouth. And there was something else.

It wasn't one cat standing in the shadows, but two. The second was covered in fluff. She was gray, with a pretty, fluffy face and twinkling green eyes. May blinked, disbelieving. But she would have known the face anywhere, no matter how many years had passed.

Dusty and covered in sand, Somber Kitty had found his way back to May.

And so had Legume.

Chapter Twenty-six

Pumpkin and Mag

The days after the cats' arrival back at the Colony, strangely, were some of the best May could remember having. She had never felt more capable, or more in her element. She asked some North Farm spirits to work shaping bows, and passed out as many silver arrows as she could spare. She asked the Risk Falls spirits to make slingshots and sacks full of mini spiky deathballs for everyone who didn't have a bow. She set the house ghosts to sewing capes for everyone, at Beatrice's instruction. Everywhere May turned, someone had a question for her about the upcoming battle, and she had almost all the answers.

- Goblins are especially susceptible to show tunes.
- The best way to shoot a silver arrow is to believe in what you are fighting for.
- Zombies are ruthless but easy to confuse.

The only answer she didn't have was what really waited for them beyond the Platte of Despair, and how they, a jumbled group of about fifty spirits, would ever defeat it. The fear loomed, but something else hung above the last of the realm's Free Spirits. It was courage.

May moved about with a spring in her step and a song on her lips, watching with a secret smile as Somber Kitty and Legume bounced about the tunnels of the colony like twin rubber bands, leaping out at each other from hiding places, biting each other's ears, tapping each other's faces lovingly with their paws. Somber Kitty had never looked less somber. Only occasionally would he deign to leap onto her lap anymore, and when he did, May would scratch his ears and think to him: *This is what it feels like to really belong.*

Somber Kitty, fearful of being made into a sacred idol, studiously avoided the Egyptians, trying to make himself as inconspicuous as possible by holding his paw up to cover his face whenever they drifted past him. Always eager to learn something new, he had inexplicably apprenticed himself to the North Farm spirits to learn carpentry. Whenever he could tear himself away from Legume, one would find him in the workshop, using his mouth and paws to assemble tiny wooden toys in record speed, despite his lack of opposable thumbs. As a gift for Legume, he even made a tiny rolling mouse—a mini replica of one he had seen outside the city of Ether. Legume purred in admiration.

Each night May, Bertha, and Lexy climbed to the Colony roof and surveyed the scene below, and every night the great shadow hand crept closer to the Colony, reaching and grasping. Finally, one night, when the hand seemed to be only a few miles away, Bertha let out a smelly sigh.

"Well, girls," she said, "if we're gonna go, we gotta go now."

They leaned on the railing and stayed quiet for many minutes afterward, watching the last of the free land of the Ever After slip away.

That night, though she didn't know exactly why, May asked Pumpkin to cut her hair.

"I never liked it, you know," she said.

"Too fussy for you," Pumpkin agreed.

"Yeah." May swallowed. She nibbled her lip nervously. She had been working up to something for many days now, and this was the perfect time to say it. Her heart fluttered with shame.

"Pumpkin," she told him, "I'm sorry for what I said, before, during the meteor shower."

"It's okay," Pumpkin said, looking down at his feet awkwardly, then sitting beside her on the bed. "It's not a big deal."

"Well." May kicked her own feet in the air, back and forth. "It kind of is a big deal. It was a really horrible thing for me to say."

Pumpkin shrugged. "It was the truth."

"No, it wasn't!" May gushed, grabbing his cold fingers. "How can you say that?"

Pumpkin, tugging at his crooked bottom lip thoughtfully, appeared to be unswayed. "It's okay. I mean, I wish it was different. You know." He waggled one hand in the air helplessly. "The spirits of Risk Falls are good at taking risks, and the Egyptians are good at building. The undead are good at surviving." He hunched his shoulders forward a little bit, sinking. "House ghosts aren't good at much. That's just the way it is."

May felt a thick knot in her throat. How could she tell him how much he mattered? "I don't see any other house ghosts but you, Pumpkin. Who else would have been brave enough to come this far?"

"Even the Shakespeare Song & Dance Revue doesn't want me," he said, and sniffed. They were both silent for a while.

"I was good at something once," he finally said.

"What's that?" May asked.

"Watching over you." He looked at her, and a tiny, sad smile played on his white lips. "When you were just a baby, and a little girl, living in White Moss Manor." He nodded, his eyes wide and sad. "I was really good at that."

May squeezed his cold hand again.

"But you're not a little girl anymore, I guess," he whispered.

May didn't know how to answer. "I'll always need you," she finally said. "Please don't give up on watching over me."

Another sad smile spread across Pumpkin's big mouth. But it was one that, May could tell, was only meant to make her feel better.

Somber Kitty had taken to sleeping on the easy chair, curled up with Legume. And so May and Pumpkin fell asleep with May's head on Pumpkin's shoulder, like two peas in a pod. Like two spirits who could never be separated.

Chapter Twenty-seven

The Beginning of the End

The next day a ragtag group of about twenty Live Ones and thirty spirits—some drifty, lopsided ghosts, some somber-looking specters, a gaggle of luminously glowing boys, a dimly lit, pumpkin-headed house ghost—set off across the Nothing Platte, headed northeast.

They dodged in and out of abandoned villages, keeping as far from the shadowy hand of Bo Cleevil as they could. As they made their way farther north, several of them kept looking back over their shoulders at the world they were leaving behind.

Finally, after days of traveling, they came to a place where the clear dusky air of the world they knew met the thick fog that marked the beginning of the Platte of Despair. A low moaning seemed to whisper through the air. And if that wasn't enough, a tiny green kiosk, broken and decrepit, sat at its very edge, a sign above its one window announcing WELCOME TO THE PLATTE OF DESPAIR. TURN BACK.

May drifted to the kiosk. On its dingy front door was a wooden hand clutching a fistful of papers, a sign above reading TAKE ONE. May did, the hand loosening its grip as she slid one of the papers out, and then tightening again after giving a brief thumbs-up sign.

Welcome to the Platte of Despair, final frontier of the Ever After. Certain doom awaits you if you continue forward. The rest of the brochure was just black, but for a pair of red eyes at the bottom of the back page. The eyes blinked at May. She shivered.

She glanced back at the fog. They couldn't see more than a couple of feet into it. Anything could be waiting for them in its white, drifty depths. "It doesn't look . . . *so* despairy," Beatrice offered, trying to sound bright. Pumpkin whimpered.

May scanned the empty horizon behind them, as if the Lady might show up after all and tell them it was safe to pass. But there was nothing. Everyone looked to May, waiting for her decision.

She peered back into the Platte. "Well," she said, stepping back from the kiosk, and then stretching a foot into the fog. "I guess we—"

"We go!" said Fabbio, raising one finger and sweeping between her and the door with a great show of bravery.

Suddenly a loud creak came from inside the kiosk. And then the door burst off its hinges, knocking Fabbio onto the ground and landing on top of him with a thud, followed by the thuds of several spirits falling out on top of it.

"I told ye to stop tickling me with yer mustache!"

"I can't help it if ye've got sensitive skin!"

"Get off me! Ye're makin' me foot fall asleep!"

"Mama mia! Help me!"

The group of knaves lying on the ground in a knot looked up then and seemed to notice for the first time that they were making a spectacle of themselves. Gwenneth, Peg Leg Petey, and some other knaves slowly stood up, brushing themselves off. Fabbio scrambled out from under the door and brushed off his uniform indignantly, then looked around surreptitiously as if hoping no one had noticed. Gwenneth scooped her foot from the ground and stuck it in her pocket, giving Petey a death glare.

May pulled her bow off her back slowly, stringing an arrow and pointing it at the knaves. "Leave us alone," she growled. Somber Kitty, trailing behind her, leaped in front of Legume protectively.

The knaves, eleven in all, jumped behind Peg Leg Petey, who waved his rough, calloused hands in front of his dimpled face. "It's not like that, lass. We didn't come to catch ye. We came to *join* ye."

"And that ain't no way to greet a friend!" Gwenneth added indignantly. May scowled at her, and she hopped back behind Petey.

"We been waitin' on ye three days," Petey explained. "'Course, Skippy is no longer with us. Ye saw the vamps nab him." He bowed his head respectfully, then continued. "Lucky the rest of us are masters at hidin' in even the most pressin' circumstances. We figured ye'd be coming up this way sooner or later. We wants to throw in our lot with ye. Make a go of it."

"You're lying," Lucius said.

"Mew," said Kitty, agreeing completely.

Petey drew circles in the dirt with his foot, sweating profusely as he looked at May's arrow. "I can see as you might have a reason or two not to trust us." He stuck a finger in his nose, then wiped it on his shirt. "But ye see, there ain't nothing or nobody left in the Ever After. *We're* all that's left." He swiped a tear from the corner of his eye. "And I says to the others, I says, we might as well go and help that little May Bird, *Book of the Dead* saying she's gonna save the realm and all. We'd like to have a friend like you. And ye see . . ." He pulled something out from under his arms and showed it to her. It was his book, *How to Win Friends, Influence Specters, Have Good Manners, and Find Buried Treasure* by Duke Bluebeard, Esquire. Petey nodded to it. "It says the best way to gain a friend is to be a friend."

"And you think Cleevil might have some treasure locked up too," Lucius finished.

Petey hesitated, then gave May an embarrassed, gold-toothed grin. "Maybe just a tad."

May and the others looked at one another. Lucius shook his head. But Bea nodded hopefully. Pumpkin gazed at the shiny spectacles hanging around Petey's neck, spacing out. Fabbio twirled his mustache, still wearing his most common expression, indignance.

"Oh, and we brought something we thought might help." Gwenneth reached into a deep sack hanging off her shoulder and pulled out two overflowing handfuls of balloons.

"What in tarnation are those for?" Bertha Brettwaller asked, emerging from the group.

Gwenneth grinned. She reached into her sack again, this time pulling out several vials of dark, oily seawater.

"Well," May said, gazing around the group. "We're not exactly in the position to turn down help."

Petey grinned and floated up to May, taking her hand and

giving it a hard shake, his dimples sinking deep into his chubby cheeks. "All fer one and all fer oneself, hmm?" He squinted thoughtfully. "Or something like that."

May replaced her bow on her back. "Something like that," she replied. She peered back proudly at the spirits behind her. And then the group, containing the very last of the Free Spirits in the Ever After—good and bad—drifted forward into the fog.

Chapter Twenty-eight

The Hole in the Floor of the World

*L*a, la, la, la, la, la, la, la, la, la."
The Free Spirits had been drifting for what seemed like a day or more. With no way to see very well, it was impossible to tell if they were drifting in the right direction. Two or three hours before, they had had to change course after bumping into a large boulder, chiseled into the shape of a skull and crossbones, that they had already come across earlier in the day. It was the only landmark they'd seen.

Fabbio zipped along far in front of the group, cutting a commanding figure and singing an old Italian army song filled with lots of *la, la, la*'s for all the words he didn't remember. His singing was almost as bad as Pumpkin's was good. Somber Kitty, lying cuddled with Legume in Pumpkin's arms, let out meow after meow, looking like his old somber self.

"Maybe this is what the Platte of Despair means," Lucius muttered under his breath.

The moan in the air, very quietly, said things like *left, right, right, turn, left*, so that May couldn't think straight.

"I think that's something up ahead," May said, hopeful and a little wary of what it might be.

As they got closer, the shape took a more specific form. A familiar one. A few more seconds, and it was obvious.

It can't be . . . , May thought, her stomach churning.

But it was. It was the same skull and crossbones from before. There, in one corner, was a place where the rock had been chipped. It was unmistakable.

"We've been going in a circle again!" she cried.

Fabbio twirled his mustache and looked about, bewildered. "This is not my fault," he said in a low, even voice.

Pumpkin flopped down dramatically on top of the skull. "Well, I'm not going any farther until *someone* figures out the right way."

Somber Kitty sniffed curiously at the bottom edges of the rock. Legume licked behind his ears.

"Maybe the 'despair' part of the Platte of Despair is that it never ends," Beatrice offered helpfully. But it didn't make anyone feel better.

"Dude, this is a total downer," Zero piped up from behind her.

Pumpkin heaved a dramatic sigh. He was now totally splayed across the skull, his head hanging upside down. "We'll never even get to fight the battle we're going to lose."

They were all silent for several seconds, thinking.

"Meay."

Everyone looked at Somber Kitty.

"Meay, meay, meay."

He flapped his tail thoughtfully, staring holes into May.

"Dude, I think your cat's trying to say something," Zero said.

May gazed at Kitty, then at the rock he'd been sniffing. She began to examine it. She examined every inch of it, for any secret buttons, or knobs, or levers. One never knew. But there was nothing. It was exactly what it appeared to be. A lifeless, dull rock. Somber Kitty and Legume looked at each other, and May could swear they were rolling their eyes.

"Well, if we try heading this way . . . ," she suggested, pointing in a random direction into the fog.

"Meay."

She looked at Kitty again. He made a big show of sniffing the rock.

May leaned on one hip and gazed at it, trying to see it in a different way. When she'd been smaller, and working on her inventions, the best way to come up with something new was to let her thinking go sideways. She tried that now.

Skull and crossbones . . . , she thought, remembering old treasure maps she'd read about in stories.

By this time, Somber Kitty had begun to make big arrows in the sand with his paws, all pointing at the boulder.

"Maybe this is what happens when you reach the northern edge of the realm," Lucius suggested. "You keep pushing toward somewhere but you just don't go anywhere."

Pushing . . . , May thought. "Push," she said.

"Huh?" asked Pumpkin, lifting his head from its flopped-back position.

"Let's try pushing the rock. There's got to be something hidden underneath. Maybe a map or . . . something. I don't know."

Everyone looked dubious. But they gathered on one side of the boulder, and Pumpkin leaped off, and on the count of three, they gave a great heave.

At first nothing happened. But then the boulder slowly began to move. And slowly, slowly, what lay underneath revealed itself.

"Keep pushing," May breathed.

With one final heave, the boulder moved completely out of the way, and everyone fell back panting and staring at the ground.

What lay there was a giant hole, dark and deep, but flickering with white light.

Somber Kitty and Legume let out loud hisses. Several spirits knelt beside it and peered inside, amazed into silence. May crouched, leaned forward onto her fists, and looked down.

The hole was in the sky. Or rather, the hole led into the air. They were looking down through a thin crust of land into a wide-open valley below—as if they were looking down on the world from the clouds. But the world below wasn't like the Ever After, dim and dusky.

May had seen it before. She had seen it painted in the glass in the great uppermost hall of the Eternal Edifice. And she'd seen it in her mind a million times since then. But she still wasn't prepared for the sight. It wasn't like anything she had ever imagined.

The dark sky flashed with thunder and lightning. Rocky mountains rose up in all directions, glinting darkly—one peak sweeping to within twenty feet below where they crouched. A deep, wide crevice bit its way between them, far below May and her friends. And spanning the crevice was what at first looked like a stone castle straight from a storybook—black as pitch, its dark spires reaching into the sky, its windows flickering with yellow light. But as May looked closer, she could see that the castle wasn't stone at all. It was carved out of an enormous tree stump, as tall as the Eternal Edifice itself, rotten and decayed, full of holes that had been turned into windows, cracks that had become doors. And at the very top, in the farthest stretch of its highest height, was one window far above all the others, glowing, not with yellow light, but an eerie red glow. A glow the color of Bo Cleevil's eyes.

"Dude, it's like Dracula's castle, only"—Zero scratched his head—"like, a million times bigger. And worse. And . . ."

Beatrice nudged him. Pumpkin had begun to shake violently, whimpering.

In the busy streets that wound and crisscrossed down the mountainside outside the castle, they could make out moving figures—and these separated themselves out into spirits, hundreds of thousands of them, many of them in chains. "It looks like every spirit in the realm is here!" May whispered, hope surging up within her. "They're still okay!"

Among the spirits moved darker ones, poking, prodding, herding. Dark spirits. Somber Kitty let out a low groan and looked at Legume protectively.

Suddenly a great blotch swooped underneath them, making them all duck backward. When they crept forward again, they could see there were several dark creatures circling the air—vampires keeping watch.

May eyed the rope tied to Peg Leg Petey's belt. She looked

down at the distance between the hole and the peak below. Then she began untying the rope and wrapping it around the skull-shaped boulder.

"What are ye doin'?"

"We're going to lower ourselves down," May said, making a knot and testing to see if it was solid.

"Ye can't be serious about goin' in there," Petey warbled, backing up.

May peered around at all the faces surrounding her. Each face seemed to ask the same thing.

"I . . . ," Bertha said, sucking on her teeth nervously. "Do you wonder if we might not be ready for this, honey?"

May, shocked, felt her resolution falter. She studied the Free Spirits. Even the Colony of the Undead looked petrified. She peered down into the hole again, at the fearsome future that awaited them if they chose to face it.

Maybe they were right. Maybe they weren't ready.

But the question was, if not now, when? Time had run out.

"We're ready," she said, nodding, hoping she looked determined, but trembling inside. If she couldn't give them courage for what they had to face, no one would. It was their only chance. "We can do this. I know we can."

Without letting herself hesitate a moment, she lowered the rope into the world below, tugged on it hard to test it one more time, and looked around the circle. "We're going down there. The only question is, who's going down first?"

There was a moment of silence.

And then someone moved forward.

Somber Kitty crept to the edge of the hole, his entire body

trembling. "Meow," he said, his voice disappearing into the blackness below.

And then he did the last thing any of them expected. He turned and ran.

May shot up. "Kitty!"

In a flash, Legume had leaped up after him, and both cats raced into the distance, fading into the fog.

The last thing May saw of her cat was his tail waving behind him, and then he was gone.

Chapter Twenty-nine

A Warrior Queen

On the rocky mountaintop above Bo Cleevil's castle, the spirits painted each other with glowing war paint, so they all looked like skeletons, even the ones who already were skeletons. It had been Pumpkin's idea. He had always had a flair for the dramatic.

They stayed up the whole night, the knaves gathered in a rowdy circle passing around a bottle of That's the Spirit spirits and swapping tales of their greatest heists, the Risk Fallsers drumming on bongos and singing hula songs, the luminous boys playing hide-and-seek among the crevices, giggling and cheating. May sat off a ways, on a rock in a quiet spot, overlooking the castle below.

Sitting in the dark, she could hear Lucius's laughter and Fabbio's booming voice. She wondered where Somber Kitty was right now, and if he was okay. She stared at the castle in the distance below, at the glowing red light of Bo Cleevil's room way up top, and wondered about him. What was he doing now?

May imagined that the spot at the top of his castle had to be the loneliest spot in the world. Worse than any kind of lonely she had ever been. Though right now, that was hard to imagine.

"Hey." May started. Pumpkin's ghastly big head poked around a rock in front of her. "Ghouly Gum for your thoughts."

Pumpkin held out a pack of Ghouly Gum, but May waved it off. "No thanks."

He floated over and sat down next to her, plucking at the pebbles on the rocky ground, then looked at her. Feeling Pumpkin's eyes on her, May's lips started to tremble, and, seeing that, his did too. She looked away, up at the dear yellow flop on top of his head.

Then a loud, gabbling sound drew their attention downward. A horde of dark blotches was moving out of the castle gates, spreading upward into the mountains to the south. It looked like thousands of dark spirits, scattering to the four winds.

May's insides began to flutter with fear.

"They must be leaving for the Cleevilvilles," Pumpkin said, expressing what she was already afraid of. Afraid, but not surprised. She thought of Earth, of all the people she knew, Claire and the lady who ran the thrift shop in Droop View and Sister Christopher and of course, most especially, her mom. They were depending on her now too. It was almost enough to make May crumple up like a piece of paper. But she didn't crumple. She stood.

"You look like someone I saw once," Pumpkin said. May looked down at herself, with her death shroud, her glowing bathing suit, and her painted skin. She imagined she was the very picture of the girl they had seen in the stained glass at the Eternal Edifice. She imagined she was the very picture of the girl she had seen in the caves underneath the Petrified Pass. She imagined she looked like a warrior queen.

As the group on the mountain quickly readied themselves to depart, there was a final burst of emotion. Peg Leg Petey admitted to Guillotined Gwenneth that he had always had a crush on her, at which admission she scowled and tried to shoot him with seawater, which had Petey ducking and hiding for his life. Fabbio confessed that he sometimes cheated at Uno, which everyone already knew.

Lawless Lexy, claiming she had been meaning to give Bertha something for a long time, handed her a long, thin box wrapped in fuschia. Bertha unwrapped it eagerly, then stared at the gift, bewildered to find a solitary white toothbrush. Lexy wiped a tear from her eye. "Use it," she said. "Please."

Several Egyptians burst into tears. Zero planted a kiss on Beatrice's cheek, making her turn bright red. Fabbio hugged a skeleton to his breast, exclaiming, "I tell you what I tella my men in the Alps. We're gonna be okay." The skeleton did not look very reassured, considering that Fabbio's men had died of frostbite.

Lucius drifted up to May and stared at her, then at the ground, kicking his feet. He looked at her for a long while, and May's ears went itchy, wondering what he was getting at. But finally he only thrust out his hand and pinched her arm. "Ow!" she squeaked, grabbing the spot where he'd pinched and watching him float away. Out of the corner of her eye, she could see Bertha blowing into her cupped hand and smelling it, still looking bewildered.

There was a final rush of hugs, and the last spirit May found herself standing face-to-face with was Pumpkin.

They looked at each other for a long moment. Pumpkin smiled a crooked smile.

"If we don't come through . . . ," Pumpkin began.

"If we don't come through," May said, "thank you for being my best friend, Pumpkin."

Pumpkin's lips began to tremble, and he couldn't say anything at all. May folded herself into his long, gangly arms and held him tight. "I love you very much," she whispered.

"I love you, too," Pumpkin said, pulling away and wiping a tear from his eye. It was funny. Looking at him now, May couldn't imagine ever having been scared of him at all.

They pulled on their capes and picked up the chains they had brought, following a plan they had reviewed one last time the night before. They chained themselves to one another in long rows, just like the spirits below. They readied their two mummy captives, repeating their threats to unravel them if they didn't cooperate. And then they began the trek down the mountain.

They were spotted long before they reached the valley floor. One vampire began to circle above them, and the others followed, like vultures.

The gates loomed up ahead, etched with screaming skulls that let out howls when they saw the spirits approaching.

May reached back behind her and held Pumpkin's long, trembling fingers under her cloak.

And then, with a great creak, the gates began to open.

That night, on Earth, Claire Arneson had a sleepover, complete with cheerful chatter, popcorn, and scary movies. Bridey McDrummy closed the Droop Mountain Shop & Spend five minutes early to sneak off with her boyfriend. Weather forecasters in twelve states predicted cloudy skies. Presidents and prime ministers in the Western Hemisphere lay down their heads but couldn't sleep, worried over politics. People in Hong Kong hit the snooze buttons on their alarm clocks, reluctant to go to work. In Briery Swamp, West Virginia, Ellen Bird spent another night lying awake with the lights on, lost in grief. The ground was broken for a new mall in White Sulphur Springs, five towns away, by men working the night shift.

The people on Earth, full of their own worries, joys, cares, and hopes, had no idea what was on its way. They went about their business, laughing, crying, talking, sleeping, dancing, worrying—living. Only the crickets and the trees sensed the danger in the air—flowing with the night breeze, whispering down from the stars—and feared.

Part Three

Scared of the Dark

Chapter Thirty

In the Heart of All Bad Things

A trail of captives wended its way through the gates of Bo Cleevil's fortress, two mummies leading them. Like so many, their eyes were downcast, their spirits dim.

The gates closed behind May and the others with a sickening thud. The scene that opened up before them was even worse than what it had seemed from above. The pathways winding up the dark hills to the foot of the great castle were paved with bones, each engraved with intricate patterns. Arching on either side of the narrow, bony streets were dark, dead trees, all twisted into the shape of a spirit in a long trench coat and a wide brimmed hat. *Cleevil*, May thought. The dark spirits, still numbering in the thousands even after the departure of so many, leaped and danced across the area, prodding prisoners with their spears, growling and snarling, their gaping mouths dripping with drool. And the whole scene was lit by flashes of lightning in the dusky sky. May could feel her chains rattling as all the Free Spirits—connected in a row like dominoes—began to quiver with dread.

May studied the chains around her wrist and her waist.

They were connected so that they only *looked* locked, and could fall off easily. She hoped the shivers passed.

Everywhere there were spirits in chains, from every walk of life—tribesmen with bones through their noses, gaggles of sad, lost-looking schoolchildren, ancient Egyptians, Babylonians, Vikings, geishas, monks, showgirls, cabaret dancers, one corpulent character, incredibly large, his head adorned with a crown of thistles . . .

"Ghost of Christmas Past," Pumpkin whispered, still trembling. Then he added, slightly lower, "I wonder if he brought any presents with him."

"Pumpkin, shhh!" May knew that when Pumpkin got nervous, he sometimes tended to babble.

"I should have stayed in the Pit of Despair. I had a great life there. A pool, a lorelei, a . . . Hey, is that Marilyn Monroe?"

"Pumpkin!" Fabbio, next in line behind him, hissed.

All around, spirits cried and sighed. Those who weren't crying had their eyes hopelessy and sadly downcast. Without exception, every one of them was part of an assembly line, putting bits of plastic together.

"What are they doing?" May whispered to Bea, who was in front of her.

"Bo Cleevil's fortress is the universe's largest exporter of tchotchkes," Bea whispered back barely audibly. Tchotchkes, May remembered her mom explaining once, were cheap things people bought that they didn't really need. They were the exact opposite of handcrafted North Farm blankets, and fine silver arrows, and everlasting cookies. They had no beauty or purpose. People only bought them to *have* them. May remembered something John the Jibber had once said, about why he hoarded treasure. To *have* it.

When someone fell behind, or stepped out of line, they were picked up and carried into the castle.

May looked up toward the castle, then peered upward to where it disappeared into the sky, thinking of Bo Cleevil, way up top. "I've got to make my way in there," she whispered. Their plan was to make it close to the castle, and for May to somehow slip out of the line unnoticed, and sneak inside, while the others got ready for . . . whatever came next. From the fifty or so ghouls guarding the gaping, rotten doorway—hundreds of balloons announcing BO CLEEVIL IS NUMBER ONE! tied to the door handles—she could see they should have come up with a different plan.

May peered around, thinking. But suddenly, she saw something that drove all thoughts from her head. It was a familiar figure among the sea of faces. By the way she felt Pumpkin jerk behind her, she knew he had seen it too.

Somewhere in the middle of one of the assembly lines, his head downcast and his antennae drooping, stood Arista the beekeeper. Only he was not the Arista May knew. He was slouched, and broken, and dim.

"A—a—," Pumpkin sputtered behind her.

"Pumpkin, shhhh." She could tell Pumpkin was using every last bit of strength he had not to squeal.

And then she felt the tug, stronger this time. She turned just in time to see Pumpkin's eyes cross and his hands flutter up in the air. And then he fainted dead away, falling right on top of Fabbio.

One after the next, and in quick succession, the Free Spirits went down like dominoes, their chains flying off their wrists, their robes thrown into disarray. Within seconds they all lay splayed on the ground on top of one another, water balloons and slingshots and arrows tumbling onto the dark ground.

May, pulled down with them, felt her robe fly open. Her glorious black bathing suit—full of supernovas and galaxies—was revealed, her sparkling arrows gleamed. All around, the dark spirits stopped what they were doing. Prisoners everywhere looked up from their tasks.

In the moments that followed, May knew she had to think fast. She looked back toward the castle. There was only a moment to decide. She would run for it.

The world behind Bo Cleevil's gates burst into chaos. Vikings leaped from their worktables and pulled ghouls' hair. Vampires chased Vegas showgirls, who'd decided to make a run for it while still chained together. The knaves, always resourceful, jumped up from the ground and chased a group of goblins with their water guns. A group of Risk Fallsers sprang to action, running to and fro, unraveling a gang of mummies.

Thousands of spirits rose up from their chains and began to turn on their captors. And their captors, fierce and fearless, fought back.

In the din, May unclasped herself from Pumpkin. She leaned over him and took his face in her hands. He was just coming to, blinking at her dazedly. "Hide!" she said, knowing he could never handle a battle such as the one they were beginning to fight. And then she turned and ran toward the castle.

She unleashed her arrows as she ran, each shot true, turning dark spirits to stone everywhere they appeared and pulling her arrows from them as quickly as she'd shot them. Finally she verged on the dark, gaping door of the castle, deserted now that its guards were deep in the fray. She looked over her shoulder to check once on her friends. Fabbio was running from two goblins throwing their shoes at him. Lucius was piggybacking a zombie. Beatrice was flinging screaming skulls from behind a tombstone. Pumpkin, having taken May's advice, was nowhere to be seen. May breathed a sigh of relief.

And then she felt the coldness of the castle breathe onto her back, and the relief faded. She took a last shot, hitting one of Fabbio's pursuers. And then she took two steps backward and disappeared inside.

Chapter Thirty-one

In the Castle

The great doors creaked behind her and May turned just as they slammed shut. She swallowed, then looked around, lowering her arrows. She was in a great hall, smelling of old wet wood and lined with giant root threads.

She could still hear the battle raging behind her, muffled and seeming far away. Somewhere farther within the castle she could hear a mournful howling. The cool, musty air sat on her arms. She felt that somehow Bo Cleevil knew she was here. There was an air of waiting all around her. As if the castle were a breathing, living thing, watching.

At the end of the hall was a great stone archway. May approached it slowly, looking this way and that, wary of what might emerge from the shadows. But she passed safely to the end of the hall, where, under the archway, a flight of stairs stretched downward into darkness. May backed up and peered around. There was no other doorway, no other hall, no stairs leading up. She put her hand against the wall and slowly drifted downward.

Click-click-click, tap-tap-tap, tap-tap-tap.

May kept close against the wall as she found herself

moving closer and closer to the sounds coming from below. She reached a soggy wooden landing and carefully peered around the corner, into a great dripping room, where hundreds of shadows moved in the dimness. She could just make out . . .

Those couldn't be what she thought they were. . . .

But yes, it was all too real. Bo Cleevil's basement was filled with monkeys.

Monkeys tapping away on typewriters.

May emerged a little farther into the room, puzzled. The monkeys kept their eyes on their typewriters, too busy to acknowledge her, though occasionally one of them scratched under his armpits, unable to help being a monkey after all. She drifted up to one of their desks and lifted up a huge pile of papers.

My One Thousand and First Bestseller, by Bo Cleevil

May shook her head in disbelief, laying the papers back down. She gave the monkey nearest her a gentle pat on the head, and then she continued on, toward another door-way at the end of the room. Holding her arrows aloft, she drifted through it and into a room full of wooden stair-cases, stretching in every direction—up, down, sideways, left, right.

May, thinking of the battle raging outside, knew she had no time to waste. She zipped up the staircase nearest to her, but it ended in a ceiling two stories above. She raced back down and tried another. This one ended in a window leading to the outside.

May tried ten staircases before she found one that led to a long wooden hallway, ten flights up. The soggy floor was dotted with large rotted holes. She wove her way around them, as quickly as she could, then stopped short.

She could hear voices, somewhere far below, singing. She strained her ears to hear what they were saying.

"One billion three hundred thousand seventy-two bottles of Slurpy Soda on the wall, one billion three hundred thousand seventy-two bottles of Slurpy Soda . . ."

May dropped down onto her belly, splaying her arms out to hold her bow and arrow, and peered into the hole, her black hair falling down on either side of her face like curtains.

She could just make out, maybe five stories down, the tops of a group of ghostly heads.

"Hey, who's up there?" one of them shouted. May Bird gasped, ducked back, and then crept forward again. Maybe it was someone who was on her side. "May Bird," she called tremulously. "Who's down there?"

"May Bird, May Bird, May Bird," she heard them all mutter to one another. And then a cheer went up.

"Shhhhhh!" she hissed.

"We heard you were going to save us. But we didn't believe it!"

May gulped. "Are you okay?"

"If you call being trapped for all eternity okay." Laughter echoed up toward her. May didn't think it was very funny. But she guessed they had to have some way to pass the time.

"How many are you in here?"

"Thousands, trapped all over the castle."

Thousands more! There was loud whispering below, and then the voice spoke up again.

"Copernicus wants me to tell you we'll spread the word you're here!" the spirit shouted.

May nibbled her bottom lip nervously, thinking of all those spirits, throughout the castle, who'd be ready and waiting to be rescued. "Listen, I need to find my way to Cleevil!" she shouted.

"Choose the seventh hall to the right!" somebody yelled. May sat up and looked around. There was no hall but one. Below, the voices resumed singing.

She floated on, this time into an enormous room, full of glinting gold and silver and jewels. There were golden statues, a gilded treasure chest marked PROPERTY OF BLUEBEARD, a gleaming sapphire the size of her head. Surrounding the room were several hallways. May, realizing what she was supposed to do, chose the seventh hall to the right, and soon found herself in a room full of carnival rides. She let out a surprised, saddened breath. It was the Carnival at the Edge of the World. Bo Cleevil had stolen it and locked it up in a room.

There were countless more rooms like this, full of wonders May could have never guessed at, and some she had already seen. There was a room so immense it contained the zipping stars that Bo Cleevil had stolen from the sky. A sign above the door read THIS VIEW COPYRIGHTED BO CLEEVIL ENTERPRISES, LLC. Here, lights bounced off May's face as if she were at a disco. Another room was full of the beautiful magnolia flowers of the Lady's North Farm tree, wilted and brown.

May stood, staring at their wilted beauty. She thought she

had begun, finally, to understand Evil Bo Cleevil. It wasn't enough for him to see beautiful things. He wanted to have them only for himself. What made a soul want to take so much from everyone else.

Mooooooaaaaaaan.

May started, and turned. The moaning that had accompanied her, faintly, since she'd entered the castle was now suddenly much louder. She peered down the dark, wooden tunnel from whence it seemed to come.

"Hello?" she ventured, her voice wavering. "Are you hurt?"

Mooooaaaaan.

It seemed, at that moment, like the saddest sound in all the world.

"Do you need help?" she whispered.

She stepped forward. And suddenly the ground beneath her moved, and she was flung backward, and her bow and arrows went flying off into the darkness. She found herself trapped in a cart of some sort. The floor of the hall before her disappeared, revealing a set of tracks stretching ahead into the darkness.

INTRUDERS FORBIDDEN!! A sign flashed brightly just above her head. HAVE A NICE DAY!

May tried to scramble out, but it was too late. She was rolling slowly forward, and then the ground began to tilt downward, and the cart accelerated, ascending just slightly over a rise. May's stomach dropped out as the cart slowly took an edge that seemed to drop off into nothing, and then it tilted forward, revealing the breathtaking scene below—a great room, hundreds of stories deep, walled with stained glass on all sides, like the inside of a church. For the moment that the cart tottered above it all, May could make out the scenes on the glass—all of a dark figure with glowing red eyes, reaching toward her. In another moment she was hurtling downward. She felt like her cheeks were blowing backward off her face.

The cart flew, down, down, down, and just as May thought it would crash right into the ground it reversed direction, turning upward again, hurtling at top speed, zooming up, up, up, impossibly high, what seemed to be as high as the very top of the castle, zipping into a square opening gleaming with light and mirrors. Etched along the mirrors were the words I AM THE FAIREST OF THEM ALL. And then the words were gone, and May was hurtling toward a big black wall that gave way just as she was about to hit it.

Booming laughter sounded all around her, shaking the cart and the tracks.

"MAY BIRD!" a voice—*his voice*—boomed.

And then the wall opened up in front of her.

She had only a second to gasp. And then the cart stopped short and flung her right out of the opening. May was suspended in the air for a moment, miles above the ground below, with nothing to grab on to but empty space. She could see the tiny figures far beneath her, fighting on the ground. And then she was plummeting to the world below.

Chapter Thirty-two

The Meaning of Lost

May didn't just land on the ground. She landed *in* the ground. She lay there for a few moments, blinking up at the dark sky. Was she dead?

She tried her arms and legs, found she could wiggle them, then reached up to pull herself out of the hole she'd made with her landing. She crawled out, stood up on wobbly legs, and began to float again, not an ache or pain in her entire body. Of course! She was dead! Nothing could hurt her!

She turned around, gaping at the hole in the ground where she'd landed, the same size as her body. It looked like a snow angel. She smiled, full of giddy relief. She wanted to leap up and down with joy.

But it took only a moment to snap back to reality. It started with a specter in a jumpsuit being flung across her line of vision. She looked around.

The Free Spirits were being beaten badly.

Everywhere, spirits that had risen up in revolt were stuffed into wire cages, their arms and legs dangling out helplessly. Zero and several other of the Risk Fallsers were bound together by a length of fiery rope, struggling to get free. The knaves had turned tail and were trying to climb up the great gates to escape, only to be plucked off one by one by a horde of goblins. It seemed that the number of dark spirits had multiplied by twenty, and they were quickly overcoming their enemies, like a tidal wave. May could see Lucius, far off in the crowd, surrounded by a group of zombies, his fists in front of him gamely, making a show of being unafraid, but clearly trapped.

"No," she whispered.

And then a crackle overhead drew her eyes up into the air far above. A long, thin line of black mist had begun to coil there, like a snake, darkening the already dark sky.

May reached for her arrows, her hand brushing against something slimy. In a moment the sliminess gripped her, and she swiveled just in time to see a ghoul before he wrapped his arms around her and lifted her into the air. May kicked and writhed. "No!"

Beside her, she could see that another ghoul floating down from the castle had her bow and arrows and was breaking the arrows in two, one by one. He got to the bow last. May struggled helplessly as he gave her a toothy, drooly smile and snapped it in half.

As she was carried toward the castle, May could see Lucius in between two goblins, being swung back and forth like a jump rope. Fabbio and Beatrice had been tied, back to back, and were being rolled along the ground. All around, their companions were meeting similar fates. As May squirmed to no avail, the Lady's words echoed in her ears: *You will fail*.

A great cheer began to bubble up from the dark spirits. May felt herself being swept in the direction of the castle.

Chapter Thirty-three

An Ancient Trick

"H ggglbblbl."

"Grrblblble."

May didn't speak ghoul, but she was pretty sure the ghouls were discussing whether to eat her now or lock her up and eat her later. She barely registered the low rumbling that had begun to shake the ground beneath them until the ghoul that was carrying her lost his footing and stumbled forward.

The ominous rumbling grew louder, and the ground shook more violently, until all the spirits—good and evil—were tumbling into one another, landing in scattered knots. Screams and howls erupted everywhere. And then, suddenly and mysteriously, the shaking stopped. For a moment everyone was silent, staring at one another, bewildered. They all looked up at the sky, where the dark mist had begun to circle tighter and tighter.

The dark spirits, collecting themselves, gabbled and laughed. "Hbblblgblbglbge," they all shrieked to one another, which in English means, "Now they're really in for it."

But another tremor drew their attention, not to the sky, but to the great black gates of the fortress. The skulls etched on its surface began to contort and howl.

Whatever was making the earth shake was coming from out there. The dark spirits' laughter evaporated.

Suddenly there was a huge crash as something made an enormous, oddly shaped indentation in the metal gates. There was a moment of eerie silence, and then another crash. The gate gave way completely, caving in with a groan. The thing that was waiting behind it came smashing through.

Everyone watched in awe as it reeled in toward them, fifty stories high at least, its enormous head rearing far above. And then it came to a halt. The ghouls scratched their heads. The goblins muttered amongst themselves. It was a moment of complete and utter shock.

Only May and a handful of ancient Egyptians had an idea of what it might mean. Breathless, May gazed at the structure from the bottom up—past the wheels, the body—her eyes lighting on something very small moving way on top. She squinted. A moment later she was sure.

A solitary figure perched majestically on the nose of the giant wooden mouse, gazing on the scene below like a conquering warrior.

The tiniest sound issued from its mouth. "Meay."

And then the bottom of the wooden mouse burst out from its hinges. And out poured . . .

. . . horses, ducks, monkeys, elephants, kangaroos, snakes, two-toed sloths, tigers, antelopes . . . every luminous animal spirit the Ever After contained. It was like the "Old MacDonald Had a Farm" of the dead.

• • •

The screams of the dark spirits could be heard for miles. Every ghoul, goblin, zombie, and vampire dropped what they were doing and ran, pouring around the castle, trying to find places to hide. The animals followed, full of righteous fury, stampeding every dark spirit in their path until they were all stuck deep into the dirt, their arms waving for help, perfectly flat.

Everywhere, dark spirits ran crying for their mommies.

Above them, the dark mist spread across the sky, circling wildly.

At six p.m. on the planet Earth, just after dusk, a strange news bulletin appeared on channel seven. According to several eyewitnesses, the reporter said, a mummy had lurched right into the middle of Prickly Valley's Pig Pickin' Jamboree and made off with the pig.

Everyone thought it was a joke.

By seven p.m., similar reports had begun to come in from all over the world, and people weren't so sure.

In Tokyo a gaggle of goblins invaded a Bill Blass trunk sale and picked out several nice things before chasing the attendees into the streets. In northern California a troop of ghouls stumbled into a vegetarian potlatch and ate one of the participants. In Mexico City, Mexico, several vampires were seen bursting from the graves of a local cemetery and heading straight for the nearest taco stand, scooping up several unsuspecting tourists in their wake to use as toppings.

Far above, the star known as the Ever After flickered and went out.

By the time calls started pouring in from panicked shoppers in Fennhaven, New Jersey; Green Willow, Wisconsin; and Pleasantville, Florida, the world had begun to realize that the reports were all too real.

Zombies had invaded the malls.

Chapter Thirty-four

A Bird at Last

Reaching for her arrows, and remembering with a pang that they were gone, May watched the chaos erupt all around her. A loud whistling drew her attention upward. The black swirling mist in the sky had whipped itself into a violent frenzy that was beginning to take a familiar shape—stretching itself downward into a kind of funnel. May's stomach flopped. She leaped out of the way as a rhinoceros stampeded past her, a babbling ghoul clinging to its horn for dear life. Up by the castle entrance, she spied a goblin trying to bribe a llama with a pair of Harry Winston earrings. Gorillas were untying the captives in droves. Somber Kitty was directing the animals from atop his perch. And about twenty feet away, a trembling yellow tuft poked out from behind a particularly out-of-the-way boulder.

She surveyed the vast array of spirits on the ground, unaware of what was happening above them, then peered toward the castle doors again. There, the BO CLEEVIL IS NUMBER ONE balloons bobbed wildly in the swelling breeze. May took a deep breath, looking at the forbidding sky above once again.

But there wasn't time for anything else.

• • •

Minutes later she was ready.

She had tied her shoe to one of the doorknobs, then tied the balloons to herself, one by one, until finally she was floating, her body straining hard against the shoelace that held her anchored.

She looked up into the sky, taking a deep, ragged breath. And then she swooped down awkwardly and untied her shoe, sending it flying off. Or rather, it was she who went flying off—up, up, up into the air, the world getting smaller and smaller beneath her. She didn't hear the tiny questioning "meay" that issued from Somber Kitty's mouth as he watched her soar upward. And she didn't see that one creature, with a crooked, squash-shaped head and a trembling yellow tuft, saw her from the ground and crept out from behind his boulder, running for the castle doors.

Soaring upward, and utterly alone, May didn't see that help was on the way. She was a bird at last.

Chapter Thirty-five

The Bridge of Souls

May's hands ran along the cold, rotten wood of Bo Cleevil's castle, controlling her ascent with clutching fingers and keeping her eyes on the swirling sky above. Her heart was in her throat as she saw the red glow of Cleevil's window approaching, and then she was upon it, and in a split second she was shoving her hands out to grip the windowsill, pulling with all her might to drag herself inside. And then she was scurrying to untie herself, peering into the red dimness for the slightest hint of movement.

There was nothing. The room was empty.

As the Eternal Edifice had been filled with colors and light, the walls of *this* room were obscured in dark, dense shadows. The room contained only an elaborately set table. At the end of the table sat a shiny red apple on a plate. And in the middle lay a thick book. May didn't have to look closer to know what book it was.

She drifted toward it, looking this way and that, wondering. She reached out her hand, and the book, all on its own, flew open, its pages flipping wildly.

"You want to know if it still says what it did," a voice said out of the darkness. May swiveled around, backing up against the table. "About you saving the world."

May stood perfectly still, peering about, unable to see anyone. There was a sound of air moving, a whisper of fabric. She swallowed, shrinking back farther against the table. Out of the corner of her eye, she spotted a dark, rotten doorway. She slid in that direction.

"You might want to take a look out the window first."

May peered in that direction.

"Why?" she asked.

There was no answer. She gave the doorway one more longing look, then floated, ever so slowly, toward the window. And then she froze in horror.

The dark mist filling the sky had swirled itself into a full-blown tornado, as tall as the castle itself. May rushed to the windowsill to peer down at the world below. The tornado's tip was tearing along the valley, picking up spirits in its wake and swirling them into the sky.

"No!" May choked. As she watched, the spirits on the ground, both good and bad, were swept up into the storm. The great wooden mouse, which looked toy-size from so far above, rattled on its foundations before it, too, disappeared into the swirling clouds. The tornado was slowly becoming a great circle of whirling, moaning spirits.

"It's been fun, watching you try so hard."

May swirled around. The voice had come from just behind her, but there was no one there. A whisper continued in her ear, blowing her hair back. "All that time you thought I wasn't there. On the train through the Hideous Highlands, cabin one seventy-eight . . ." May's stomach twisted. "Sitting on the back of the boat in the middle of the Dead Sea, catching up with your friends. At the Colony of the Undead. In the hotel in Hocus Pocus. Those long talks with that pitiful, useless house ghost of yours. I was there for all of it. Just over your shoulder. Watching. Laughing. It was all just so thoroughly enjoyable."

May was speechless. Chills crept up and down her body.

"I was there in Briery Swamp, too. I heard the things you whispered to your cat when you thought no one was listening."

May shook her head.

"Oh," the voice rasped, making May's ear tingle, a smile weaving its way through the words. "Poor thing. Don't you understand? I am everywhere. When you hear something go bump in the night, that's me. When you feel the hairs stand on the back of your neck, I'm there. I am the thing that lurks in the shadows. I am the starless night. Tell me, little speck, are you afraid of the dark?"

May felt something move behind her and turned to see a shadow forming in the window. It solidified into a figure in a dark hat, standing on the windowsill and staring out at the world below. He turned to her, his red eyes glowing menacing from beneath the brim of his hat. Otherwise, his face was covered in shadow. He was slouched, almost forlornly.

"Did you ever notice that you think something will make you feel different, but you end up feeling the same?" he asked.

May didn't answer. But she thought of Pumpkin, and how with all his realm-wide fame he still felt small. She thought of ᵛ, in Briery Swamp, she had wanted so badly for the other kids to really notice her. But when they had, it hadn't felt very good at all. She thought of herself, a true warrior now, and still as scared as she'd ever been.

"The truth is, I'm an evil ruler success story," Bo Cleevil said. "The dark spirits love me. I control the entire world of the dead. Earth"—he waved a hand in the air carelessly—"will be a piece of cake." He sighed theatrically. "And still . . . I feel . . . *empty.*"

The red glow of his eyes dampened just a little. May bit her lip, calculating what might happen if she made her move now. She could try to push him out the window. She could . . .

He pointed a hand toward her, and May felt a viselike shadow wrap its way around her arms, squeezing her tight. She struggled but couldn't move so much as an inch. It took her breath away, how easily he held her.

"Please don't think about interrupting again," Bo Cleevil said. His eyes flamed red once more, and bored right into her. And then his body relaxed again. "Where was I? Oh yes, empty. But then I look at someone like you. So *full* of thoughts, and colorful ideas . . . unique." His hot-coal eyes drifted to her short black hair, her skeletal disguise, her sparkling black bathing suit and pajama pants. "I find it quite amusing that you spent so much of your time in Briery Swamp trying to hide it. Trying to give away what makes you strongest." He tilted his head thoughtfully.

"Like I said, you and I are not so very different. We're both singular sorts of spirits. We're both alone. Together we could be something else entirely. You would never feel small again."

May was speechless. Her eyes flew to the tornado outside, to where her friends were being swept away. There was no Lady No Somber Kitty. No anyone standing beside her. But strange she didn't feel alone at all. She felt like everyone who'd loved her, and every brave thing she'd ever done, stood behind her, holding her up.

And May realized that something had changed for her, something she hadn't noticed before. She was scared. But she wasn't scared of being scared anymore. "I'm not alone," she said.

She squirmed suddenly, sliding out of the shadowy grip, and instead of lunging toward the door, she lunged toward Bo Cleevil. The moment she did, the shadowy grip wrapped around her again and lifted her into the air.

"Well, that's very nice for you," Bo Cleevil said, "because things are about to get very scary." With a wave of his hand, he lifted her higher into the air, stepping down off the windowsill and moving toward her. A great flapping sounded behind her, and they both turned to see *The Book of the Dead*, its thousands of pages frantically flipping by themselves.

Bo Cleevil stayed where he was and looked up at her. "So tell me, if you know so much, how do you think it ends?"

At that moment something flashed through the room. Bo Cleevil stumbled backward in surprise as the shadows were broken by a blinding white light. A great wind swept through the window, blowing them sideways. Dangling, May lifted her arms in front of her eyes to shade them, squinting to see what was.

The Bridge of Souls sat in the middle of the room, gleaming ghtly, leading up to where the ceiling had been. Only now, ead of a ceiling, there were countless stars in a dark sky. The d howled and whistled hollowly.

Still holding on to her, Bo Cleevil laughed. "I guess that settles it," he said. He turned back to her and smiled. "It's a shame, really. But I guess it's your turn to cross."

He advanced upon the bridge. May had only a moment to think. She swung herself forward, tumbling toward him and landing on his shoulders, piggyback-style. Bo Cleevil plucked her off like lice and flung her onto the ground, then leaned toward her. As he reached for her, she grabbed his hat, pulling it off, and scrambled backward. But when she saw what was underneath it, she froze.

Nothing. Nothing but a pair of coal red eyes, drifting in space. His face was emptiness itself.

In another moment he had her by the arms, and she was lifted up again. He carried her to the very edge of the bridge, where she dangled, amazed and helpless. May bucked and wiggled wildly, her eyes drifting across the bridge, to the blackness beyond. "No!" she cried.

"Good-bye, little speck."

He dangled her a moment longer, winding up to throw her. The wind sucked at her hair and her shroud like a vacuum cleaner. It howled through the room. The chairs around the table went flying across. The plates blew forward, smashing on the floor.

And then there was a loud crash behind them, and Bo Cleevil swung back to look.

The door had flown open, and all in a rush there was a figure hurtling through it, long limbs flopping every which way, white face pale as moonlight, yellow tuft flopping wildly. Pumpkin's wide black eyes focused on the scene before him: Bo Cleevil, the bridge, and May dangling before it. He charged.

And barreled right into Bo Cleevil.

May went flying sideways. She rolled across the floor, righting herself just in time to see Pumpkin and Bo Cleevil, tangled together like strings, go barreling onto the bridge. The wind roared to a deafening pitch, sweeping them in a great gust all the way across.

"Pumpkin!" May yelled.

But as she lunged toward them, the room exploded in white light. Before May's eyes, the two separate figures began to change, turning into balls of the brightest white she could imagine. And the lights exploded like fireworks and shot up, up, up, impossibly high, until they were only tiny pinpricks far above. They shot upward for a second more, and then the wind around May died completely, the room went quiet, and the two white lights came to rest far above, twinkling.

May, her head craned back on her neck, watched in awe.

Beside her, the bridge vanished as quickly as it had appeared, but the scene above did not. Bo Cleevil's castle lay open to the sky. A sky that held two newborn stars.

May stood for a moment, disbelieving, afraid, devastated, and amazed.

And then she heard an odd sound coming from outside the window. She rushed to see the tornado twisting its way back from the mountains and slowly dissipating, losing its speed, its tight gray spiral become loose and misty.

And from it, all sorts of objects had begun to fall.

May squinted, trying to make it out. There was a man in a chef's hat. A specter in a toga. A ghost with horns and a beard. May peered up into the air. Thousands of spirits were falling from the sky, squealing, shouting, cheering. There were loud *yee-haw*s and *woo-hoo*s as the ghosts and specters of the Ever After free-fell back to land.

It was raining spirits. A smile crept onto May's lips.

And then a sound behind her pulled her attention to the table. Though every other thing that had been resting on the table had blown off, *The Book of the Dead* still remained where it had been. It lay open, its pages flapping in the soft breeze.

May drifted to it slowly, glancing up from time to time at the sky above, full of too many feelings to understand. She stopped at the edge of the table, leaning toward the book just slightly, as if she were wary of what she would find there. When she saw it had opened to the *P*s, a lump formed in her throat. Finally the pages stopped turning. Her eyes lit on the right-hand side. Halfway down the page was a name, buried between Poltergeist Polly and Puss and Eyeball Pie, that no one had ever bothered to look for: Pumpkin. Next to it was a single entry.

Only slightly more responsible than
May Ellen Bird for saving the world.

Chapter Thirty-six

Love, Patience, Grace

Knock, knock, knock.

May was the first one up in the Colony of the Undead that morning. She padded down the tunnel, wondering who could be at the door so early.

She was wary as she opened the door a crack and looked outside, bewildered at what she saw. Outside on the sand there levitated a troupe of elaborately dressed characters. They wore puffy velvet hats with feathers, brocade vests, and poofy pantaloons with tights underneath. One of them had a curly mustache and a pointy beard.

"We are looking for a worthy house ghost by the name of Pumpkin," said the one with the beard. "Wouldst thou help us to locate him? We are in dire need of his talent."

May studied the one with the beard. He looked familiar. School-textbook familiar. And then it hit her who he was. And her throat started to go lumpy. And she wanted to laugh and cry at the same time. And instead of doing either, she invited them in for tea and explained to the Shakespeare Song & Dance Revue just why Pumpkin wasn't there, and what had happened to him, and what he had done for the land of the dead.

Three months had passed since the day the sky had rained spirits.

Since then, the Ever After had not magically gone back to the way it had been. Nothing broken heals that quickly. It would take time, and patience, and hope—and slowly, over years, it would begin to grow back into what it had been. Maybe it would even be a little better. Already townsfolk had gone back to bustling about, sometimes laughing, sometimes crying, moaning, sometimes complaining. All the things that made the land of the dead lively. Now animals roamed free over the Ever After. Some spirits had even learned what change was like. And they'd found out it really wasn't so bad.

Already, all over the realm, Cleevilvilles had begun to fall into disrepair, and colorful, messy, lopsided towns had begun to sprout around the decay. Nobody missed it when the occasional town mischief-maker stole one of the PARDON OUR DUST! signs for a souvenir to keep in their rooms, to remind them of the bad old days.

A sapling that had sprouted in the wasteland of Bo Cleevil's fortress was rumored to be growing into a beautiful magnolia tree. The Lady of North Farm was said to have returned to the snowy valley behind the Petrified Pass, and spirits had begun to try to recall whether she was good, or bad, or a mixture of both.

The dark spirits, with no one to tell them what to do (because they were not the brightest bulbs in the cosmic basket) had returned from their one wild night out on Earth only to scratch their heads and look at one another blankly. By the following evening, they had all slunk back down to South Place—which they'd always preferred to Earth anyway. For years to come, they would tell stories about the one night they had terrorized the living, repeating themselves over and over, whenever there was a slimy ear to listen. Most of their grandghouls found it horribly boring.

At the Colony of the Undead, there had been picnics under the zipping stars, and parties in the main hall, and slumber parties on the newly rebuilt roof. Bertha Brettwaller, Lawless Lexy, and the rest had been overjoyed when May, Beatrice and Isabella, Lucius, Fabbio, and the cats came to stay. There had been many long nights spent talking over their adventures. And many quiet hours together where they thought only of Pumpkin and didn't say much at all. Weeks had turned into months. And now, here May stood, telling the Shakespeare Song & Dance Revue something that still hurt too much to say.

When she was finished relating the news, the troupe fell silent and lifted off their caps, bowing low.

"He had the sweetest voice I've ever heard," the man with the beard, Will (as he asked May to call him), said. The troupe, which had been captured by Bo Cleevil on the same day they'd auditioned Pumpkin, all murmured agreement. And then, sadly, they trailed off into the desert again.

It was that day that May decided. It was time to go.

There were some things May was still not brave enough to do. When it was time for good-bye, Lucius stood there for a long time like they both wanted to say something, but neither of them did.

Finally, Lucius spoke, "So we'll see each other again," he said unsurely. May nodded. She reached out as if to touch his hand, but at the last moment, she only pinched his shoulder and stuck out her tongue at him. He laughed, ducked forward as if to tackle her, but at the last minute turned to peck her on the cheek. In another moment, he'd zipped off in a brilliant ball of light.

Fabbio refused to come say good-bye. Beatrice accompanied her to the edge of the Nothing Platte. She held her hand tightly and tried to look like she wouldn't cry.

"We'll be down to visit soon," she said. "We'll take the train, once it's up and running." They smiled at each other, remembering an earlier train journey together. They hugged, and then they let each other go.

In Belle Morte, May did chores and helped Arista tend to the bees. She felt closest to Pumpkin there. And she felt she owed it to Pumpkin to look after these things, though she found that she was always making holes in Arista's bee suits, or setting all the bees free by accident. Often she'd stop her chores to watch Somber Kitty with an absent smile. He was now the proud father of six ghostly kittens, who traipsed about Beehive House and its gardens, ignorant that animals had ever been banished, or that there had ever been a spirit called Bo Cleevil. May watched him sometimes, out of the corner of her eye, proudly guarding his brood. Often she wondered if he ever thought of home like she did. There was never a moment when home, and her mom, were absent from her thoughts. But she held her chin up.

Still, sometimes she stared at Pumpkin's grave and thought about trying to use it to haunt the Earth, so she could have just a glimpse of her mother, even as a ghost. But she didn't want to end up as a lost soul. She never wanted to be lost again.

At night she and Arista sat by a cozy fire in the parlor, often in companionable silence, Kitty, Legume, and their kittens lounging all over their laps. Sometimes they talked about Pumpkin, and all the funny things he used to do. Sometimes when May stood in the backyard after Arista had gone to sleep, she was sure she could feel someone watching her, and she looked up at the zipping stars. She wondered which one he was. These days, she knew she had to be her own guiding star. But sometimes, she liked to imagine, Pumpkin helped.

It was on just such a night that the first extraordinary thing in a long time happened to May Ellen Bird. She was staring up at the stars when she saw something strange crossing the sky. For a moment she gazed at it absently, merely curious. And then she realized it was getting closer and closer. It began to resemble a giant ball of fire headed straight for Belle Morte.

"Get inside!" she yelled, scooping up a handful of kittens and ushering Somber Kitty and Legume indoors, where Arista was puttering about the kitchen.

Outside, the ground began to shake. They all dove under the kitchen furniture. And then, as quickly as it had begun, the shaking stopped. They all looked at one another, scared witless, May's mind leaping to a million possibilities. But none of her conjectures prepared her for what she saw when she finally crawled up to the window and peeped outside.

There in the front yard sat a long white rocket, emblazoned

on one side with the word NASA. No sooner had this begun to sink in than a round hatch opened with a hiss, and a familiar figure came tumbling out: Bertha "Bad Breath" Brettwaller. Seeing May in the window, she did a jolly little jig and motioned her to come outside. May zipped out into the yard, gaping in awe. But Bertha took it all in stride.

"Well c'mon, girly, we ain't got forever anymore. Hop in."

"Hop in?" May repeated hollowly.

"You know. Pick it up, hit the road, git a move on! I had to beg 'em to stop for ya. They're in a real hurry to get back to Earth and tell 'em about this here world of ghosts. Apparently it's still a big deal down there to discover a star filled with the supernatural."

May felt a moment of elation, her heart soaring as high as the tip of the rocket. And then, in the same moment, it plummeted. "But Bertha . . ." She looked Bertha up and down, her shoulders drooping as she then looked at herself. "Somber Kitty and I . . . we're dead."

Bertha let out an annoyed sigh. "Ya think I ain't got that covered? Sheesh, I only been leading the Ever After's living spirits for a hundred-odd years. Ya think I ain't got secrets?" She pulled a little velvet pouch out of her overalls. The label on the front read REJUVENATING RE-LIFE POWDER, HANDCRAFTED BY THE SPIRITS OF NORTH FARM.

"Honey," Bertha said, leaning in conspiratorially, "I've died twenty-three times since I got to the Ever After. This stuff costs an arm and a leg, but *whoooee*, is it worth it. If ol' Lawless saw me dead, I'd never live it down. Now get on in and you can sprinkle it on on the way."

May turned to Arista, who'd watched the whole scene, and looked him a question.

"Zzzz, my dear, I'd really rather you go. You're a much better warrior queen than a house ghost."

May was packed within minutes. She packed her and Kitty's death shrouds carefully away. How long had they been gone? A year? More?

She hugged Arista good-bye, then Legume, and the kittens, one by one. Bertha was already in the rocket, waving at her through the window to get a move on. "C'mon, Kitty," she said, drifting for the door.

"Meay."

May turned.

Somber Kitty stood by Legume's side, looking at her plaintively.

May put down her knapsack, walked back to him, and knelt down. Why hadn't it even occurred to her? How could she not have thought of it? Her bottom lip began to tremble.

"You want to stay?"

Kitty looked at her, then at Legume. "Meay," he said again.

May looked back over her shoulder at the shuttle. Could she leave Somber Kitty behind? Was that even something she had in her? She swallowed the lump in her throat. She looked back at Kitty.

She pulled him close to her and felt his soft warmth. She rubbed her cheeks against his dear fuzz. She whispered secrets to him that only the two of them had shared. She wanted to go on holding him forever. But finally she set him gently on the ground and stood up.

"Tell the others I'll see them again sometime," May said to Arista, hugging him again. And then, feeling like she was ripping a piece of herself off and leaving it with Kitty, she followed Bertha through the hatch, not looking back. They buckled themselves in. The engines began to rumble. The hatch began to close.

And then there was a loud screeching, and a dark blob came flying through the door, just before it shut.

"Kitty!"

May pulled Kitty to her tight and rubbed her tears on his fuzz, which he didn't like. She tucked him carefully into her seat belt. They both looked out the window at what they were leaving behind.

"It's gonna be a wild ride," Bertha said, grinning at them from her seat ahead. She laughed in May's face, and May winced, only to be pleasantly surprised. Bertha's breath was minty fresh.

The engines rumbled madly, and they blasted off. All of them shook as the shuttle ascended higher and higher into the air. It was another minute or so before May could gather herself enough to look out the window again.

The star got smaller and smaller beneath them. And then it was only a round, glowing dot. And then it was surrounded by a mass of countless other stars.

And then there was no looking back at all. Because the Ever After was only a speck, lost in space behind them.

Epilogue

Fame was a funny thing.

Amidst the world's realization—thanks to NASA—that ghosts not only existed, but had their own world several light-years away, May Bird got lost in the shuffle. Only one reporter came to interview her, in the library of White Moss Manor with her mom, who wore a MAY BIRD WENT TO THE LAND OF THE DEAD AND ALL SHE BROUGHT ME WAS THIS LOUSY T-SHIRT T-shirt, and he left looking sorely disappointed. There was too much about saving the world, and not enough about dead celebrities. The story never ran.

That was fine with May and her mom. They preferred it that way.

There were nights baking cookies, and nights curled up on the sofa watching movies, nights where they sat with Somber Kitty between them and talked for hours, May's mom listening raptly to May's stories of the Ever After, her eyes widening to hear of the Carnival at the Edge of the World, or twinkling at tales of Pumpkin's goofy antics, or rolling as May tried to recite, from memory, one of Fabbio's poems, or one of the knaves' songs of thievery. At times like these, Kitty purred with contentment, and they knew that for the moment, he'd stopped thinking of Legume just for a little while, happy to be exactly where he was.

But nothing in the world stays still. They broke ground for a group of sparkling white condominiums in the spring following May's return, and downtown Briery Swamp was suddenly aflutter with newness, all of it encroaching on the trees. And then it seemed like no time at all before May was in high school, and trading nights on the couch with her mom for nights under the stars with her friends, cold bleacher afternoons with classmates at football games, colorful costume parties with lots of new people to meet, cozy poetry readings at the Y'All Come In Café in Hog Wallow. Shyness still crept up on her sometimes when she least expected it, but then she only smiled at it, like an old reliable friend. She even found that when she showed parts of herself that seemed strange or wild, people usually smiled, and then shared crazy ideas of their own. It seemed, when all was said and done, that all souls were a little wild, in some way or another.

Outside White Moss Manor, the woods slowly receded, no longer waiting and whispering outside the house's windows, full of secrets. The condos that took their place stretched all the way through what had once been a great brier patch, and slowly grew around a lake that had reappeared, a tiny black circle in a cloudless clearing.

When May went off to college, Mrs. Bird and Somber Kitty sat on the porch rocking many nights, wondering what she was doing at that moment and hoping she was happy. She was studying for her final exams the night that Somber Kitty passed away, in his sleep. He had been dreaming of pyramids. May rushed home the next day, and she and her mom buried him in the backyard, right next to Legume. May did not wear black. She did not need to wear something to touch the grieving in her heart.

That year, several inhabitants of the Briery Swamp condos went missing. Nobody blamed it on the lake. But several families began to move just the same. With a surreal quickness that no one could explain, the houses became vacant, and the development, bankrupt. And the buildings began to be eaten up by the woods again. In a few years' time, they would be gone completely.

Only White Moss Manor would remain.

Briery Swamp had always belonged to the woods, anyway.

One dusky evening, far above, in the Ever After, a fuzzy, bald, big-eared spirit arrived in Belle Morte after a long journey. He was surprised to find Fabbio, Lucius, Bea, and Isabella already there. They had all, over the years, gravitated to Belle Morte, as if in anticipation of something they couldn't yet name.

They made a merry group, playing hide-and-seek in the village, helping Arista with his bees, playing Scrabble around the cozy kitchen table, until Fabbio usually got caught cheating.

And still at night sometimes, Somber Kitty would sneak out to the edge of the yard, padding out under the sky full of zipping stars, and stare across the horizon, as if he could just make something out, coming across the desert. He sometimes sat all night, flapping his tail expectantly, waiting.

Waiting for May Bird to come home for good.